Tommy Sullivan is a FREAK

Meg Cabot is the author of the phenomenally successful The Princess Diaries series. With vast numbers of copies sold around the world, the books have topped the US and UK bestseller lists for weeks and won several awards. Two movies based on the series have been massively popular throughout the world.

She is also the author of the bestselling *Airhead, All American Girl, All American Girl: Ready or Not, How to Be Popular, Tommy Sullivan Is a Freak, Jinx, Teen Idol, Avalon High,* The Mediator series and the Allie Finkle series as well as many other books for teenagers and adults. She and her husband divide their time between Florida and New York.

Visit Meg Cabot's website at
www.megcabot.co.uk

Books by Meg Cabot

The Princess Diaries series

The Mediator series

All American Girl
All American Girl: Ready or Not

Airhead
Avalon High
Avalon High manga: The Merlin Prophecy
Teen Idol
How to Be Popular
Jinx
Tommy Sullivan Is a Freak
Nicola and the Viscount
Victoria and the Rogue

For younger readers

Allie Finkle's Rules for Girls: Moving Day
Allie Finkle's Rules for Girls: The New Girl
Allie Finkle's Rules for Girls: Best Friends and Drama Queens

For older readers

The Guy Next Door
Boy Meets Girl
Every Boy's Got One
Queen of Babble series
The Heather Wells series

Also available in audio

Meg Cabot

Tommy Sullivan is a Freak

MACMILLAN

First published 2007 by Macmillan Children's Books

This edition published 2009 by Macmillan Children's Books
a division of Macmillan Publishers Limited
20 New Wharf Road, London N1 9RR
Basingstoke and Oxford
Associated companies throughout the world
www.panmacmillan.com

ISBN 978-0-330-44407-1

5 7 9 8 6 4

A CIP catalogue record for this book is available from
the British Library.

Typeset by Intype Libra Ltd
Printed and bound in the UK by CPI Mackays, Chatham ME5 8TD

For Benjamin

Many thanks to Beth Ader, Jennifer Brown, Barbara Cabot, Sarah Davies, Michele Jaffe, Laura Langlie, Amanda Maciel, Abigail McAden and especially Benjamin Egnatz.

One

'Oh my God, what's *she* doing here?' my best friend, Sidney van der Hoff, was asking as I came up to the corner booth to hand out menus.

Sidney wasn't talking about me. She was glaring at someone at another table.

But I couldn't be bothered to look and see who Sidney was talking about, since my boyfriend, Seth, was sitting next to her, smiling up at me . . . that smile that's been making girls' insides melt since about the fifth grade, when we all started noticing Seth's even white teeth and highly kissable lips.

It still freaks me out that of all the girls in school, I'm the one he picked to kiss with those lips.

'Hey, babe,' Seth said to me, blinking his long, sexy eyelashes — the ones I overheard my mom telling Sidney's mom over the phone are totally wasted on a guy. He snaked an arm around my waist and gave me a squeeze.

'Hi,' I said a little breathlessly. Not because of the squeeze, but because I had a table of twelve (Mrs Hogarth's ninety-seventh birthday party) that was running me ragged, refilling their iced-tea glasses and such, so I was panting a little anyway. 'How was the movie?'

'Lame,' Sidney answered for everyone. 'You didn't miss anything. Lindsay should stick with red, blonde does nothing for her. Seriously, though. What's Morgan Castle doing here?' Sidney used the menu I'd just given her to point at a table over in Shaniqua's section. 'I mean, she's got some nerve.'

I started to say Sidney was wrong – no way would Morgan Castle be caught dead at the Gull 'n' Gulp. Especially at the height of the summer season, when the place was so packed. Locals – like Morgan – know better than to try to set foot near this place during high season. At least, not without a reservation. If you don't have a reservation at the Gull 'n' Gulp – even on a Tuesday night, like tonight – during high season, you can expect to wait *at least* an hour for a table . . . *two* hours on weekends.

Not that the tourists seem to mind. That's because Jill, the hostess, gives them each one of those giant beepers you can't fit into your pocket and mistakenly walk away with, and tells them she'll beep them when a table's free.

You'd be surprised how well people take this information. I guess they're used to it, from their T.G.I.Fridays and Cheesecake Factories back home, or whatever. They just take their beeper and spend their hour wait strolling up and down the pier. They look over the side rails at the striped bass swimming around in the clear water ('Look, Mommy!' some kid will always yell. 'Sharks!') and maybe wander over to historic Old Towne Eastport, with its cobblestone streets and quaint shops, then wander back and peer into the yachts at the Summer People watching satellite TV and sipping their gin and tonics.

Then their beeper goes off and they come hurrying over for their table.

Sometimes, while Jill's leading them to a table in my section, I'll overhear a tourist go, 'Why couldn't we just have sat THERE?' and see them point to the big booth in the corner.

And Jill will be all, 'Oh, sorry. That's reserved.'

Except that this is a total lie. The booth isn't reserved. Well, not technically. We just hold it open every night, in case of VIPs.

Not that Eastport, Connecticut, sees that many VIPs. Or, OK, any. Sometimes, between lunch and dinner, when there's a lull, Jill and Shaniqua and I will sit around and fantasize about what we'd do if a REAL celebrity walked into the place, like Ryan Phillippe (although we've gone off him a bit since his divorce) or Justin Timberlake, or even Prince William (you never know. He could have got lost on his yacht or whatever).

The crazy thing is, even if by some incredible fluke an actual VIP like that did show up at the Gull 'n' Gulp, he wouldn't get a seat at the VIP booth. Because in Eastport, Connecticut, the only true VIPs are the Quahogs.

And that's who the corner booth is always saved for any Quahog who, for whatever reason, might not have made a

3

reservation at the Gull 'n' Gulp during high season, and needs a table.

Shocking but true: every once in a while a tourist will wander into the restaurant who has never heard of a quahog. Peggy, the manager, had to take me aside my first day working at the Gulp last June, when a tourist was like, 'What's a quahog?'

Only they said it the way it's spelled, kwah-hog, instead of the way it's supposed to be pronounced, which is koh-hog.

And I was all, 'You don't know what a QUAHOG is???' and almost died laughing.

Peggy explained to me, very stiffly, that quahogs actually aren't that well known outside the north-east, and that people from the Midwest, for instance, have probably never even heard of them before.

She was speaking of the bivalve, of course. Because that's what a quahog is – a type of clam that, when mixed in a pot with a lot of potatoes, onion, leeks, heavy cream and flour, make for the Gull 'n' Gulp's bestselling chowder. Those types of quahogs are what Eastport has been known for since like the 1600s, practically.

Now, though, our town is known for a different type of quahog entirely. Because the Quahogs is also the name of Eastport High School's football team, which has won the state championship every year since before I was born, sixteen years ago.

Well, except for one year. The year I was in eighth grade.

But no one ever talks about that year.

It's hard to say which quahogs the town's residents are proudest of, the clams or the team. If I had to guess, I'd say it's the football team. It's easy to take a clam – especially one that's been around for that long – for granted. The team's only been on its winning streak for a decade and a half.

And the memory of what it felt like NOT to have the best team in the state is still fresh in everybody's mind, since it was only four years ago, after all, that they were forced to forfeit that single season.

That's why nobody in town questions the corner booth. Even if some local did, for whatever reason, show up at the Gull 'n' Gulp during the summer season without a reservation, he wouldn't expect to be seated in the empty corner booth. That booth is for Quahogs, and Quahogs only.

And everybody knows it.

Especially my boyfriend, Seth Turner. That's because Seth, following in the footsteps of his big brother, two-time first-team All-State defensive-end Jake Turner, is this year's varsity Quahog kicker. Seth, like his brother before him, loves the corner booth. He likes to stop by the Gull 'n' Gulp when I'm working, and sit there till I'm done, drinking free Cokes and inhaling quahog fritters (deep-fried dough with bits of clam inside, that you dip in a sweet 'n' sour sauce. This is the only kind of quahog I can stand to eat, because the dough masks the quahog's rubbery texture, and the sauce masks its total tastelessness. I am not a fan of the quahog – the bivalve variety, I mean. Not that I've dared mention this to anyone. I don't want to get run out of town).

Anyway, then, when my shift is up, Seth puts my bike in the back of his four by four, and then we make out in the cab until my curfew, which is midnight in the summertime.

So the corner booth is a total win-win situation, if you ask me.

Of course, lots of times Seth isn't the only Quahog in the corner booth. Sometimes his brother Jake – who now works for their dad's construction company – comes along.

Not tonight though. Tonight Seth's brought along Quahog defensive lineman Jamal Jarvis and his girlfriend, Martha Wu, as well as quarterback Dave Hollingsworth.

And of course, wherever Dave goes, my best friend, Sidney van der Hoff, has to trail along, since she and Dave have been attached at the hip all summer, ever since Sidney's former boyfriend – last year's Quahog quarterback, All-State most-valuable-player Rick Stamford – graduated in the spring and sent Sidney a *Dear Sidney* text message, telling her he needed his space and wanted to see other girls when he went to UCLA in the fall.

Which, if you ask me, was pretty decent of him. He could have strung Sidney along all summer and then just dumped her when he got to California – or even just gone ahead and seen other girls behind her back and not told her, and come back for Thanksgiving and Christmas vacations expecting to pick things up where they'd left off. It's not like, being all the way across the country, Sidney would ever have known Rick had his tongue in some Kappa Kappa Gamma's mouth.

Although actually it is possible – even easy – to see other people behind your significant other's back while living in the same town, without that person – or anyone else, for that matter – ever finding out. Easier, for instance, than hiding the fact that you can't stand quahogs (the supposedly edible kind).

I'm just saying.

So it was nice of Rick not to string Sidney along. I told her that at the time, even though it didn't seem to console her much. Sidney didn't really calm down until she found out Dave had broken up with Beth Ridley due to her cheating on him with this hottie from Australia she met while crewing on her uncle's parasailing charter.

So Sidney invited Dave over to her house to commiserate about their no-good exes in her jacuzzi over Boylan's Creme Soda (Sidney's was sugar free, of course). And Dave didn't even try to take her bikini top off, which really impressed Sidney.

So of course she hooked up with him.

For such a small town, a lot of stuff happens in Eastport. Sometimes it's hard to keep up.

Like right now, for instance. Because when I looked over at Morgan Castle's table and saw who she was with, I knew EXACTLY what she was doing at the Gull 'n' Gulp on a Tuesday night in high season.

And I also knew I didn't have time for the drama that

was about to erupt. I mean, I had Mrs Hogarth's birthday to deal with.

Sidney didn't know that though, and even if she had, she wouldn't have cared. I've been best friends with Sidney van der Hoff, the most popular girl in my class, since second grade, when I let her cheat off me during a spelling quiz. Sidney had been a wreck that day, on account of her kitten having gone in to get spayed. Sidney had convinced herself Muffy wasn't going to survive.

So I took pity on her and let her copy my answers.

Muffy got through her surgery just fine, and grew into a fat cat who I got to know quite well from the frequent slumber parties I attended at Sidney's house afterwards, Sidney not being the sort of person to forget a kindness.

That's what I love about Sidney.

It's all the drama I could live without.

'Oh my God, is that *Eric Fluteley*?' Sidney was totally staring at Morgan's table. 'That's even WEIRDER. What's HE doing here? This is hardly his kind of place. I mean, considering that no Hollywood casting scouts are likely to walk in.'

'Hey, Katie,' Dave said, ignoring his girlfriend's outburst. This was typical Dave behaviour. He is a notorious smoother-over . . . one of those people who is always calm, no matter what the situation – even Morgan Castle and Eric Fluteley dining together at the Gull 'n' Gulp. That's why he and Sidney make such a good couple. She's a disrupter and he's a smoother-over. Together, they're almost like one normal person. 'How you doing? Busy tonight, huh?'

'Way busy,' I said. He had no idea. This family from like Ohio or something had come in earlier, and the parents had let their kids run around all over the place, bothering Jill up at the hostess stand, throwing French fries out into the water (even though the signs on the pier supports say, very clearly, *Do Not Feed the Birds or Fish*), getting in the way of the busboys when they were carrying enormous trays of used plates, shrieking for no reason, that sort of thing.

If my brother and I had acted that way in a restaurant, my mom would have made us go sit out in the car.

But these parents just smiled like they thought their kids were so cute, even when one of them blew milk at me from a straw.

And then, after all that, they only left a three-dollar tip.

Hello. Do you know what you can buy in Eastport for three dollars? Nothing.

'I'll make this quick then,' Dave was saying. 'I'll have a Coke.'

'Make it two,' Jamal said.

'Make it three,' Seth said, with another one of his knee-melting smiles. I could tell by the way he couldn't take his eyes off me that things were going to get steamy in the cab of his truck later on. I knew the cami I was wearing had been a good idea, even though Peggy has a thing about bra straps showing and had almost made me go home to change until Jill had pointed out that *her* bra straps show

9

every single night, and if it's OK for the hostess, why not the waiting staff?

'Diet for me, please, Katie,' Martha said.

'Me too,' Sidney said.

'Two diets, three regulars, and two quahog fritter platters coming up,' I said, regathering the menus. We always throw in free quahogs for the Quahogs. Because it's good for business to have the most popular guys in town hanging out at your establishment. 'Be back in a minute, guys.'

I winked at Seth, who winked back. Then I hurried to turn in their order and get the drinks.

I couldn't help glancing in Eric's direction on my way to the soda station – and saw him staring at me over the top of Morgan's head. He had that look on his face – the same look he got when I was taking his headshots for his college apps and the stills of him for the *Gazette* during that really intense scene from *The Breakfast Club*, which our school put on, where Bender talks about how his dad burnt him for spilling paint on the garage floor. Eric played Bender, and you could TOTALLY see how Claire, the school's prom princess, would go for him.

Eric really is talented. I wouldn't be surprised to see him in the movies some day. Or some TV series about sensitive but fearless doctors or whatever. He's already got an agent and goes on auditions and everything. He almost got a part in a Daisy Brand Sour Cream commercial, but was dropped at the last minute when the director decided to go in a different direction and use a five-year-old instead.

Which I could understand. I mean, it's sour cream.

How intense do you want the guy to look about it? Even now, Eric was looking at me so intensely that Morgan, who was trying to talk to him, totally paused and looked around to see what he was staring at.

Quick as a flash, I turned my back on them and leaned down to ask Mrs Hogarth if there was anything she needed.

'Oh no, Katie dear,' she said, beaming at me. 'Everything is just lovely. Larry, honey, you remember Katie Ellison, don't you? Her mother and father own Ellison Properties, the real estate firm in town.'

Mrs Hogarth's son, who was in Eastport with his wife (and some of his kids and some of their kids and a few of *their* kids) to take his mom and her best friends from her assisted living community out for her birthday, smiled. 'Is that so?'

'And Katie takes pictures for her school paper,' Mrs Hogarth went on. 'And for our community newsletter. She took that nice picture of the quilting club. Remember, Anne Marie?'

'I thought I looked fat in it,' said Mrs O'Callahan, who, by the way, *is* fat. Although I'd tried to Photoshop out some of the excess, knowing she'd complain later.

'Well,' I said super-chipperly. 'Is everyone ready for dessert?'

'Oh, I think so,' Mrs Hogarth's son said with a wink. He'd stopped by earlier with a cake from Strong's Bakery, which we'd stashed in the back and which I was supposed to bring out while singing 'Happy Birthday'. The

Hogarths had forgotten to get candles though, so I'd run over to the card shop and picked up two shaped like the numbers nine and seven. They were kids' candles, with clowns on them, but I knew Mrs Hogarth wouldn't mind.

'Oh, nothing for me, thanks,' Mrs Hogarth said. 'I'm stuffed. That grouper was delicious!'

'I'll be right back to see if anyone wants coffee then,' I said, and hurried around the corner to the soda station, still careful not to look back in Eric's direction.

Ducking into the kitchen, I grabbed Mrs Hogarth's cake, threw on the two candles and started out again –

– and almost crashed right into Eric Fluteley, who – looking at me intensely the whole time – took the cake from my hands, set it next to the coffee-maker, grabbed me by both shoulders and kissed me on the lips.

Two

'The Gull 'n' Gulp just so isn't Morgan Castle's kind of place,' Sidney was going on, into my cellphone.

I grunted in response. I was trying to work some leave-in conditioner through my wet hair with a comb. I'd had to wash it three times after my shift in order to get the smell of fried quahog out of it.

Seriously, I don't know how Seth can stand to make out with me when I stink so much of clams.

But the stink is pretty much the only downside of wait-ressing at one of the most popular restaurants in town. Especially when you pocket forty-eight bucks in tips, like I did tonight.

Not to mention the added bonus of getting kissed by Eric Fluteley at the soda station.

'I mean, shouldn't she have been over at the Oaken Bucket?' Sidney asked.

'Totally.' I don't know what's going on with my hair. I have been trying to grow it out ever since an unfortunate bobbing incident midway through sophomore year. It's almost shoulder length now, with a lot of layers (because the stick-straight thing that works so well for Sidney doesn't work at *all* for me) and gold highlights to make it less aggressively *brown*. According to Marty over at Supercuts, I'm supposed to let it dry naturally, then scrunch it with curl enhancer to make it fuller and give it bounce.

But that only seems to work when it's humid outside or I'm in the vicinity of the Gull 'n' Gulp's kitchens.

Sidney was right, of course. The Oaken Bucket, the vegan cafe across town, is much more Morgan's scene than the Gull 'n' Gulp. I mean, the Bucket serves stuff like falafel in a pitta with hummus and avocado, and tofu stir-fry over brown rice. You won't find a single item on the menu made with quahogs over at the Bucket, that's for sure.

'There's only one reason she'd go there,' Sidney went on, in her most malevolent tone. 'And we all know what it is.'

I nearly dropped my phone. Right into the toilet, which is where the comb ended up. Fortunately, I'd remembered to flush earlier. I caught the phone at the last minute and pressed it to my ear.

'W-wait,' I stammered. 'What? We *do*?'

How could she know? She couldn't know! No one had seen me with Eric – had they?

I *knew* I should have slapped him. Oh *why* had I kissed him back? I totally wouldn't have, if I'd thought there was any chance that Seth – or Sidney – might have seen us.

But the soda station is totally hidden from view of the corner booth. And from where Morgan Castle was sitting.

So instead of slapping Eric Fluteley when he started kissing me I'd melted, exactly as if I'd been one of Mrs Hogarth's birthday candles left to burn too long.

Well, what else was I going to do? I mean, Eric's just . . . hot.

When Eric finally let me up for air though, I said, very indignantly (admittedly through delightfully tingly lips), 'What are you, crazy? Did you see who's sitting in the corner booth? The entire Quahog football team!'

Eric had replied, 'Not *all* of them. Don't exaggerate, Katie.'

'Well, the ones who'd totally pound your face in, if they saw you doing what you just did.' I really couldn't believe it. I mean, what had he been *thinking*? You do not just go up to a girl and start kissing her behind the soda station. Especially when her boyfriend is sitting just a couple of metres away.

Even if, you know, she really likes it. And wants to do it some more.

'What's he doing here anyway?' Eric had wanted to know. 'I thought you said the fire was gone and you were finally breaking up with him.'

Had I told Eric that the fire was gone between me and Seth? Probably. It had gone out pretty soon after we'd become a couple and the excitement that Seth Turner, the most popular boy in school, had picked me – ME! – as his steady girlfriend had died down.

But how can you break up with a guy who's just so . . . nice? I mean, what kind of awful person would do something like that? Break up with her boyfriend of nearly four years because he's just . . . boring?

Had I told Eric that Seth and I were breaking up? Probably. Oh God, what was happening to me? I couldn't even keep all my lies straight any more.

'Yeah,' I'd said. 'Well, I haven't got around to it yet. Obviously.'

'Katie.' That was when Eric reached over to take my hand and gazed meaningfully into my brown eyes with his gorgeous blue ones – the same blue as the Long Island Sound on a cloudless day. 'You've got to break it off with him. You know you two don't have anything in common. Whereas you and I – we're artists. We have me something special. It's not fair of you to do this to him.'

The thing is, Eric was totally right. Well, not about him and me having something special – except, you know, that I think Eric's totally hot, and a dynamo kisser.

I meant about the part where he said that Seth and I really don't have anything in common. We don't.

Well, except that I think Seth's totally hot, and a dynamo kisser too. I've thought that for as long as I can remember – well, the totally hot part anyway. I didn't know about the kissing part until the end of eighth grade, which was the first time Seth ever laid one on me, during a game of Spin the Bottle in Sidney's basement rec room after a midsummer pool party. It was like a dream come true for me – the boy every girl in school wanted actually wanted ME. We've been dating ever since.

But even so, Eric was one to talk.

'What about Morgan?' I demanded. 'How are you being fair to *her*?'

Eric didn't even have the dignity to look embarrassed.

'Morgan and I aren't a couple,' he'd said. 'So I can't exactly be accused of doing anything wrong.'

'Neither can I!' I'd insisted, even though I'd known at the time that this was sort of untrue. 'I so didn't do anything. I'm just trying to take Mrs Hogarth her birthday cake!'

'Yeah,' Eric said sarcastically. 'Just like you *so didn't do anything* today before your shift started.'

Oops! Well, yeah, so OK. I had sort of made out with Eric at the employee bike rack behind the emergency generator before work.

But whatever! That didn't mean he could kiss me while he was out with another girl!

'You get back to Morgan right now,' I'd said. 'This is a terrible thing to do to her. She's so sweet too. I don't even know why you brought her here. She's a vegan. There's nothing she can eat here except salad.'

'I was trying to make you jealous,' Eric had said, his hands going around my waist. 'Is it working?'

It was just then that Peggy rounded the corner holding an empty iced-tea pitcher. She'd stopped dead at the sight of us. Because of course patrons aren't allowed in employee-only sections, such as behind the soda station.

Or even back behind the emergency generator by the employee bike rack either.

'Is there a problem back here, Ellison?' Peggy had asked in an astonished voice.

'No,' I'd said quickly, as Eric sprang away from me. 'He was just looking for—'

'Salt,' Eric had said, grabbing a nearby salt shaker from the tray by the soda dispenser. 'Bye.'

He'd hurried back to his table while Peggy, meanwhile, narrowed her eyes at me.

'Ellison,' she'd said in a suspicious voice, 'what's going on?'

'Nothing.' I'd grabbed Mrs Hogarth's cake and held it out. 'Do you have a lighter?'

'I thought you were going out with Jake Turner's little brother,' Peggy had said in the same suspicious voice, after reaching into the pocket of her khakis and pulling out a lighter, then lighting the number nine and seven candles.

'I *am*,' I'd insisted. 'Eric's just a friend.'

A friend I like to make out with when I get the chance, I'd thought, but didn't add aloud.

Peggy had rolled her eyes. She's been managing the Gull 'n' Gulp for ten years. I guess she's seen it all. Heard it all too.

'I knew I was wrong not to make you go home and get a sweater,' was all she'd said.

Like if my bra straps hadn't been showing, I'd have somehow managed NOT to get caught kissing Eric Fluteley behind the soda station?

18

But Peggy wouldn't have told *Sidney* about what she'd seen me doing. Peggy doesn't gossip (and she busts her employees' chops when she catches them doing it).

So how had Sidney found out? No way had she seen Eric kiss me behind the soda station.

Could she have seen me outside by the bike rack earlier today?

No way. Sidney doesn't even own a bike. She never goes anywhere at all unless it's in Dave's Camaro or the white convertible Volkswagen Cabriolet her dad got her for her sixteenth birthday.

'I'll tell you why Morgan was there,' Sidney said knowingly into the phone. 'She's spying. On the competition.'

Oh God! The competition for Eric's affections? That's totally me!

Except that if Sidney knew, why hadn't she said anything to me? I mean, Sidney's not exactly reticent with her opinions, and if she found out I've been macking behind an emergency generator with Eric Fluteley, you can bet she'd have a few things to say about it. Sidney thinks Seth and I are the perfect couple and is looking forward to her and Dave and Seth and me being the It Couples of our senior year. My getting caught macking with Eric Fluteley would totally ruin Sidney's plans for the prom, et cetera.

'I mean, her sponsor's the Oaken Bucket,' Sidney went on. 'How much do you really think they're contributing to her campaign? Whereas you actually *work* for your sponsor, so they've got like a vested interest in actually promoting you . . .'

19

Oh. Oh my God.

I sagged down on to the side of the bathtub in relief. OK. So *that* was what Sidney was talking about. Not Eric. Nothing to do with Eric.

'And, seriously, does she really think anyone's going to vote for a Quahog Princess who doesn't even eat quahogs?' Sidney wanted to know.

I can't believe I almost forgot. That there's another type of quahog, I mean, besides the clam and the football team.

There's the town's annual contest for Quahog Princess. Which I'm running for.

And so is Sidney. And so is Morgan.

Which is why Sidney can't stand Morgan, even though Morgan is really sweet, once you get to know her. Which I did, because Morgan, who has been taking ballet since she was like four and is a shoo-in for the Joffrey Ballet Company in the city someday, danced Laurey's dream sequence in the drama club's production of *Oklahoma!* last spring (Eric played Jud. And let me tell you, he was the hottest, most brooding Jud ever. A lot of girls – like me, for instance – thought Laurey should have gone with Jud instead of that stupid Curly, who was played by Paul McFadden, who is kind of a sissy anyway), and I had to photograph her in it for the yearbook and the school paper.

Morgan was super nice about doing her grand jetés over and over, since I couldn't quite get the shot right with my digital Sony, and her legs kept blurring. (I finally got an excellent shot of her in mid-air, with her legs perfectly horizontal to the stage. It looks like she's flying, but she's got this calm expression on her face, almost bored, like, 'Ho hum, I defy gravity like this every day.')

Morgan's doing that same dance for the talent portion of the Quahog Princess pageant.

And can I just say that one of the things Sidney dislikes most about Morgan is the fact that Morgan's talent is way better than Sidney's, which is singing a Kelly Clarkson song – not to mention mine, which is the worst beauty-pageant talent of all . . . playing piano?

Although the fact that Morgan's got this long, skinny neck and no body fat and never talks to anyone doesn't exactly endear her to the Sidney-types of the world either. It isn't that Morgan thinks she's better than everyone, as Sidney insists. She's just really shy.

It's scandalous that Eric was using her to try to make me jealous. I am fully going to have a talk with him next time we make out behind the emergency generator.

'Oh,' I said to Sidney, laughing with relief when I finally realized she was talking about Quahog Princess and not Eric. 'I don't think she was there to spy on us. I think it's just where Eric took her. It wasn't like she could say anything. He had to have made that reservation a week ago.'

'Yeah, and what is up with that anyway?' Sidney wanted to know. 'Who makes a reservation at the *Gull 'n' Gulp*?'

Sidney, I knew, wasn't dissing the Gulp. It's just that no local would ever deign to make a reservation there, unless it was a special occasion, like Mrs Hogarth's birthday party.

Or a guy who wanted to make the girl he was currently macking with behind her boyfriend's back jealous.

'Maybe he wanted to impress her,' I said, carefully fishing my comb out of the toilet, just as there was a thump on the bathroom door.

'I'm *in* here,' I called to the thumper, who I knew was my brother, Liam, just getting home from the video arcade at Duckpin Lanes, where he'd spent most, if not all, of his nights this summer. No one else in my house was awake, since it was after midnight.

'Yeah, but since when are Eric Fluteley and Morgan Castle a couple?' Sidney demanded. 'It all seems a little too convenient, if you ask me. She's running for Quahog Princess and needs an escort for the evening-gown event, and she just HAPPENS to start going out with the best-looking guy in school? I mean, besides Seth and Dave? And then just HAPPENS to show up at the Gull 'n' Gulp on a night when we're both there?'

'I'm at the Gulp almost every night, Sid,' I pointed out. 'So are you, for that matter. I really don't think Morgan was there to spy on us.'

'Oh God, Katie,' Sidney said. 'You are *such* an innocent.'

Sidney always calls me an innocent, because even though Seth and I have been going out forever, I'm still a virgin, and Sidney lost hers to Rick Stamford two summers ago in his room while his parents were out attending the Eastport Towne Fair.

But I just don't think it's a good idea for a girl who can't seem to stick to kissing one guy at a time to start sleeping with them too. I mean, at least Sidney was sure she loved Rick (and thought he returned the feeling). I think the fact that I can't stop kissing Eric Fluteley is a pretty good sign that, as hot as I've always thought he is and all, I'm not in love with Seth . . .

. . . and the fact that I can't stop kissing Seth means I'm most likely not in love with Eric either.

Although I kind of wonder if Sidney would still think I'm so innocent if she knew why Morgan Castle had *really* been at the Gull 'n' Gulp tonight – because Eric Fluteley brought her there to make me jealous.

Not that I'm going to tell her – or anyone else – that.

Liam thumped again. I flung the comb into the sink, turned on the hot water in hopes of killing whatever germs were now growing on it, thanks to its toilet plunge, and yanked open the door.

'I'm *in* here,' I said to my brother, who, just this past summer, grew six inches in three months and now towers over me, even though at five seven I am three inches taller than Sidney, and, in fact, am one of the taller girls in my class. Especially when my hair is doing what it's supposed to and fluffing up.

'I *know* that,' Liam said sarcastically. 'I need to—'

'Then use the downstairs bathroom,' I said, and started to close the door.

'I wanted to tell you something,' Liam said, putting a hand to the door so I couldn't close it. 'If you'd quit yakking on the phone long enough to listen. Who is that, anyway? Sidney?'

23

'Hold on, Sid,' I said into the phone. Then I turned off the hot water – I'm not sure how long it takes to sterilize toilet germs off a plastic comb, but I don't want to waste water either – and said to Liam in an impatient voice, 'What?'

'Who is that?' Sidney wanted to know. 'Liam?'

'Yeah,' I said into the phone. To Liam I repeated, '*What?*'

'Oh, nothing,' Liam said with a shrug. 'It's just that I saw someone you know tonight down at Duckpin Lanes.'

'That's thrilling,' I said to him. 'Now go away.'

'OK, fine,' Liam said, turning to continue down the hall to his room. 'I just thought you'd want to know.'

'Who?' Sidney chirped in my ear. 'Who did he see? Oh my God, ask him if it was Rick. If it was Rick, and he was with Beth Ridley, I'll die. Martha said she heard Rick and Beth hooked up at Hannah Lebowitz's Fourth of July barbecue—'

'Liam,' I said. I didn't say it loud, because I didn't want to wake up Mom and Dad, who were downstairs in the master bedroom they added on off the laundry room two years ago, so they could be away from us kids. 'Who was it? Was it Rick Stamford?'

'You wish,' Liam said with a snort.

'What do you mean, *you wish?*' I demanded.

'I mean, you *wish* it was Rick Stamford and not who I'm about to tell you it was. Because when I tell you, you're going to freak.'

24

'Was it Rick?' Sidney wanted to know. 'What did he say? I can't hear him. Your phone gets the worst reception . . .'

'It wasn't Rick,' I said into the phone, while Sidney, on the other end of my phone, shrieked, 'It must have been a celebrity then! Was it Matt Fox? I've heard he's buying a summer place over in Westport. Was it Matt Fox? Ask him if it was Matt Fox!'

'It was Tommy Sullivan,' Liam said flatly.

At that, I did drop my cellphone. Fortunately, however, not into the toilet. Instead, it landed on the floor.

Where it broke into three pieces.

As it was falling, I could hear Sidney going, 'Wait, I didn't hear him, what did he—'

Then smash.

Then . . . silence.

Liam looked at the pieces of my cellphone and laughed.

'That's what I was trying to tell you,' he said. 'Tommy Sullivan's back in town.'

Three

OK, why?

That's all I want to know.

Why did Tommy Sullivan have to come back *now*, just when everything was going perfectly – to mess it all up?

The summer before your senior year is the last summer when you can actually have a good time. No stresses yet about college apps and transcripts. No freaking out about extra-curriculars or Chemistry.

And this has been the most outstanding summer of my life so far: people have finally started to realize that even though I'm the class brain, I can still be fun to party with. I've got a job I love, where I make good enough money to have (almost) fully paid off the camera I really want. I've got a fantastic boyfriend and an even hotter guy to mack with behind the emergency generator when that boyfriend isn't around . . .

So why does Tommy Sullivan have to come back NOW and ruin it all?

Liam wouldn't give me any details last night after he

dropped his little bombshell, because he was mad I wouldn't get off the phone to Sidney to listen to him. Liam's fourteen and starting his freshman year at Eastport High, and his new height totally attracted the attention of Coach Hayes, who spied Liam towering over everyone at freshman orientation and asked him if he was trying out for the Quahogs.

Since Liam – like every other guy in Eastport – practically lives for Quahog football, this totally went to his head. He's been impossible to live with ever since. And try-outs aren't even until Friday.

But I knew from experience that I'd wear him down eventually and get him to spill the details of his Tommy Sullivan stunner. Liam can't keep a secret to save his life.

Which is why, when I saw what time it was when I woke up the next morning, I said my best swear word, rolled out of bed and, without even showering first, threw on my clothes (and, OK, a tiny bit of make-up, because a girl running for Quahog Princess really shouldn't be seen in public without her mascara on), hopped on my bike, and pedalled over to the Y, where Liam's been going every day to lift weights in the hope of bulking up for Quahog try-outs on Friday.

Oh yeah. I'm like the only almost-seventeen-year-old in Eastport who doesn't have a car. I'm not one of those vegan environmentalist types who hangs out with Morgan Castle over at the Oaken Bucket or anything. I totally love meat. I just think if you live in a small town – and Eastport's only got twenty-five thousand full-time residents (though May through to August the population rises to thirty-five thousand, on account of the Summer People) – you should ride a bike around and not drive. It's better for the environment and better for you physically as well.

Sidney thinks it's weird I'm saving my money for a camera and not a car, like everyone else we know (although, to be truthful, everyone else we know got a car for their sixteenth birthday. I asked for – and received – a Power Mac G5, along with a full colour printer so I could print my own photos – although I still take my film in to Eastport Old Towne Photo if I want something really professional-looking), but there's nowhere I need to go that isn't within biking distance (except the city, but I can take public transport there), so why waste fossil fuels when I can just use pedal power?

And, unlike Sidney, I don't have to spend hours in the gym every week, since I get all my exercise from biking around.

Oh, fine. OK, true confession time: I get carsick. I fact, I get everything sick – seasick, airsick, train-sick, carsick, even raft-sick (from floating on a raft in a pool) and swing-sick (from swinging on a swing).

The only time I don't feel sick? When I'm walking. Or riding a bike.

My mom blames it on all the inner-ear infections I had as a kid. My dad – who has never been sick a day in his life and won't let any of us forget it – thinks it's all psychosomatic and that as soon as I fall for a cute enough guy I won't get sick at all when he's driving me around, and I'll even want to get a licence. For instance, so I can drive with the guy in a Ferrari through the Alps. Because, Dad says, no one can function as an adult without a driver's licence.

But, as I've informed Dad numerous times, there is no guy in the world cute enough for this to happen.

And, besides, it's totally possible to function as an adult without a driver's licence: it's called New York City, where all the great photographers in America live and work.

And guess what? They have bike paths there too.

Anyway, I locked up outside the Y and went inside to find my brother lying on a padded bench, pulling on some kind of cords that caused all these weights behind him to raise up a few inches. Not unusually, there was a cluster of fourteen-year-old girls gathered around him, giggling excitedly. Because, since word got out that Coach Hayes himself had approached Liam about trying out for the Quahogs, every fourteen-year-old girl in town has been calling the house at all hours of the day, asking if Liam's there.

Clearly, all the Tiffanys and Brittanys I've been taking messages for have figured out where Liam spends his free time – when he isn't at Duckpin Lanes.

'Excuse me, ladies,' I said to them. 'But I need to have a word with my brother.'

The Tiffanys and Brittanys tittered like I'd said something funny. I've seriously never seen so many tanned bellies in my life. Do these girls' mothers really let them out of the house dressed that way? I was betting they left wearing real clothes, then whipped them off as soon as Mom wasn't looking any more.

'Not now, Kate,' Liam said, his face turning very red.

Not because he was embarrassed, but because he was lifting way more weight that he probably should have been, to show off in front of the girls.

'Oh yes, now,' I said, and pulled on some of his leg hairs.

CRASH! went the weights behind him.

Liam said a number of very colourful swear words, and the girls scattered, giggling hysterically, but really only retreating as far as the water cooler over by the desk where they hand out the towels.

'You didn't really see Tommy Sullivan at Duckpin Lanes last night,' I said to my brother. 'Did you?'

'I don't know,' Liam snapped. 'Maybe not. Maybe it was some other guy who came up to me and asked if I was Katie Ellison's little brother, and introduced himself as Tom Sullivan. Why'd you have to do that? Pull my leg hair like that? I hate it when you do that. I could have seriously injured myself, you know.'

'*Tom* Sullivan?' For the first time since I'd heard the news that Tommy Sullivan was back in town, my heart lifted. Tommy never called himself Tom. He'd always been Tommy, since kindergarten, when I'd first met him.

Maybe whoever Liam had met last night wasn't Tommy Sullivan – *my* Tommy Sullivan – after all!

'Maybe it was someone else,' I said hopefully. 'Some other Thomas Sullivan.'

The look Liam gave me was very sarcastic.

'Yeah,' he said. 'Some other Thomas Sullivan who told

me he'd been in your class at school and wanted to know how you were doing . . . and has red hair?'

My heart totally stopped beating. I swear for a few seconds I couldn't even breathe. I could hear the rock music the Y plays over its sound system – it was on the local pop station.

But it sounded really distant.

Because there's only one Tommy Sullivan I know of who's ever been in my class at school.

And only one Tommy Sullivan I know of who has red hair.

That hair! How many times since eighth grade, when Tommy finally left town, had I seen a guy – a tourist, usually – with red hair and done a double take, my heart hammering, certain it was Tommy, and I was going to have to look into those weird hazel eyes of his, which in certain lights were as green as the Sound during high tide, and in others as amber as leaves on an autumn day, sometimes even gold, like honey – only to have the guy turn around and end up not being Tommy at all?

Phew! I always told myself when this happened.

But could what Liam was telling me possibly be true? Could my luck – where Tommy Sullivan is concerned anyway – finally have run out?

'What did you say?' I asked, sliding on to the bench beside Liam. Which was a mistake, since the cushion was slick with sweat. But I didn't care that much, since I hadn't showered yet anyway.

'When he asked how I was doing,' I demanded 'what did you say?'

'I told him you were good,' Liam said. 'I told him you were going out with Seth Turner.'

My blood went cold. I couldn't believe it. Liam had told Tommy Sullivan that I'm going out with a *Quahog*?

'You told him *that*? Why'd you tell him that?'

'What else was I supposed to say?' Liam, getting up from the bench to reach for his bottle of Gatorade, looked annoyed. 'He asked what you were up to. I told him you were running for Quahog Princess.'

I groaned. I could only imagine what Tommy must have thought about my running for Quahog Princess, an honorary title with absolutely no benefits other than that the Quahog Princess gets to ride in a convertible Chevrolet with the mayor during the annual Eastport Towne Fair parade (I fully intended to take a Dramamine beforehand if I won) and open the Quahog Festival, which takes place on the third Sunday of August.

Which happens to be at the end of this week.

And, OK, to qualify you have to have a Grade Point Average of at last three point five (which, believe me, rules out a LOT of girls at my school), and be willing to show up at a lot of cheesy events during the Eastport Towne Fair, such as the quahog-eating contest (disgusting) and the quahog races (boring. Bivalves aren't that fast).

But to compensate for all that, the winner also gets fifteen hundred dollars cash in scholarship money from the Eastport Quahog Festival committee.

Even better, the money comes in the form of a cheque made out to the recipient, which she can deposit into her personal account and then spend on whatever she wants. I mean, they don't *check* to make sure she spends it on her education.

Which, I'll be frank, is the reason I'm running for Quahog Princess.

And, OK, I know I have zero chance with Sidney running too (she couldn't care less about the money. She's in it for the tiara).

But at least I have a better chance than Morgan Castle. I mean, Morgan Castle can barely open her mouth in public, she's so shy.

Although she has a much better talent than I do. I mean, for competing in a beauty pageant.

And yeah, I realize beauty pageants are sexist and all that. But come on. Fifteen hundred bucks? Even second place is a thousand. Third is five hundred.

So even if both Sidney and Morgan beat me (which is likely), I'd still be five hundred more dollars up than I would have been if I hadn't entered (the only other entrant is Jenna Hicks, who has multiple nose and eyebrow piercings, only wears black no matter how hot it is outside, and whose mother is making her enter in order to make her socialize more with girls her own age who don't list KAFKA as their answer to Interests on their myspace page. Which, not to be mean or anything, doesn't exactly make Jenna Quahog Princess material).

Which is good, because my parents are making me cut

back my hours at the Gull 'n' Gulp to one night a week once school starts up again next month, so I will totally need the scratch.

'What did he say?' I asked. 'When you told him about Quahog Princess?'

Liam shrugged. 'He laughed.'

I felt the hairs on the back of my neck rise.

'He *laughed*?' I did not like the sound of that. At *all*. 'Laughed like how?'

'What do you mean, laughed like how?' Liam wanted to know.

'Like did he laugh like he thought it was funny,' I asked, 'or like an evil genius? Was it *ha ha ha*? Or *MWA ha ha*?'

'What is *wrong* with you?' Liam asked me, loudly enough to cause the Tiffanys and Brittanys to burst into a fresh batch of giggles, over by the towel desk.

Whatever. Let them laugh. What do fourteen-year-olds in belly-baring tanks and yoga pants know about pain? And not just the kind you get when the belly-button piercing you got illegally in the city gets infected and you have to tell your mom so she can take you to the doctor, and then she grounds you.

I mean real pain, like trying to figure out what Tommy Sullivan could be doing back in town. He and his parents had moved away – to Westchester, outside New York City, a whole other state – the summer before our freshman year . . . the same summer I'd first played Spin the Bottle and kissed Seth. They had never said they were moving because of what happened the year before. In fact, my mom, who was their realtor and sold their house for them, said Mrs Sullivan had told her they were moving so Mr Sullivan could have a shorter commute to his job in Manhattan.

But everyone had always just sort of assumed that what had happened with Tommy – and the outside of the new Eastport Middle School gymnasium wall – was a large part of why they left.

So why had he come back? It's true his grandparents still live here – we see them sometimes when Mom and Dad make us eat at the yacht club, which they belong to not because we own a yacht (Dad's boat is strictly for fishing; it doesn't even have a bathroom on it. Which isn't the only reason I won't get on it, but it's one of them), but because belonging to the local yacht club is good for schmoozing if you're in the real-estate business, like they are.

And OK, I suppose Tommy must come and visit his grandparents sometimes . . . although truthfully it never occurred to me before. Why wouldn't they just go to see him in Westchester? I mean, Eastport could hardly have good memories for him. Why would he want to come *here*?

But even if he just happened to be here because he was visiting his grandparents, why would he go to Duckpin Lanes, which is where every guy in town hangs out? That would be the LAST place you'd think someone as universally despised as Tommy Sullivan would go.

'Katie?'

I looked up, and saw Seth grinning down at me, all

melting brown eyes and sleek biceps, clearly fresh from a workout.

'What are you doing here?' he wanted to know. 'You never come to the Y.'

Which isn't strictly true. The Y is where I took my first photography class, the one that got me into cameras in the first place, even though the instructor – crabby Mr Bird, proprietor of Eastport Old Towne Photo – had hardly been encouraging.

But I let that slide, because, hello, hot guy. Who happens to be my boyfriend. Well, one of them anyway.

'Oh, I just came by to see how Liam's doing,' I said, as Seth slipped an arm around my waist and gave me a kiss. Which made me glad I'd put my mascara on. It was bad enough I still had bed-head.

Naturally, I didn't mention *why* I'd come to see Liam. In my long and varied career as a liar – which began at approximately the same time that Tommy Sullivan left town – I've learned that sometimes it's kinder to lie to people than it is to tell them the truth. Especially when the truth could hurt them. Seth can't even stand to hear Tommy's name uttered. He gets all quiet and moody whenever the subject comes up . . . even though his brother seems perfectly happy working for their dad.

Although probably not as happy as he would have been playing college ball.

So I've found it better, over the years, simply to keep mum on the Tommy front where Seth is concerned.

36

'I've been trying to call you all morning,' Seth said. 'Don't you have your cell on?'

Oops! I'd managed to snap all the pieces of my cellphone back together and had charged it up. But I'd forgotten to turn it on. I pulled it out of the pocket of my shorts and pressed POWER. A second later, I saw my screensaver – a picture of Seth, looking dreamily at me over an order of quahog fritters.

'My brainiac,' Seth said fondly. Because, even though I consistently rank top of our class, I am always doing things like forgetting to turn my cellphone on.

A second later, it rang.

'What happened to you last night?' Sidney asked after I'd answered. 'We got disconnected. I tried to call you back a million times and just got your voicemail.'

'Right,' I said. 'Dropped my phone. I had to recharge it.'

'Oh. So. Who was it?'

'Who was what?'

'Who'd your brother see at Duckpin Lanes?' Sidney wanted to know.

'Oh,' I said, thinking fast, watching as Seth started showing Liam how to use another nearby machine, while the Tiffanys and Brittanys gathered round, looking more worshipful than ever. Because, hello, Jake Turner's little brother. I didn't blame them. I'd felt the same way about him, back when I'd been starting ninth grade. Still do. Well, sort of. 'That. It was nobody. Just this guy Liam knew from football camp.'

'Why would he think you'd care about *that*?'

'I don't know,' I said. 'Because he's let this Quahog thing go completely to his head, maybe?'

'Oh, right. Well, where are you?'

'The Y,' I said. 'With Seth.' I didn't mention the whole part about having come to the Y to see my brother, not Seth, let alone the thing about Tommy Sullivan being back in town. I mean, it's not like I can tell *anybody* that. Any of my friends, I mean. They've all managed to forget that I ever even used to consort with Tommy Sullivan. I don't want to do anything to remind them of that fact.

'Oh good,' Sidney said. 'Grab Seth and go home and get in your swimsuit. The wind's up, so Dave wants to kitesurf. We're going to The Point.'

The Point is the private beach that belongs to the Eastport Yacht Club. Nobody in Eastport goes to the public beaches, because of not wanting to hang around with a bunch of tourists. Also, in the paper they're always reporting finding traces of E. coli in the water down at the public beach (caused by tourists with RVs illegally emptying their toilets into the water).

Still, given the whole Tommy thing, I wasn't exactly in the mood for the beach.

'I don't know,' I hemmed. 'I was sort of thinking of going home and practising –'

'For the pageant?' Sidney sounded disgusted. 'Oh, what*ever*.'

'– and I've got the dinner shift at the Gulp tonight.'

'So? Bring your work clothes. You can change at the

38

club. You need to work on your tan more than you need to work on that gherkin thing—'

'Gershwin,' I corrected her. 'It's "I've Got Rhythm" by George Gershwin.' I love Sidney and all, but really – *gherkin*?

'Whatever,' Sidney said again. 'Get your stuff and get to the club.'

Which is why, later that afternoon, I was stretched out on a blue and white Eastport Yacht Club beach towel, listening to the water lapping the shore (I wouldn't like to mislead anyone by saying I was listening to the sound of waves, because of course there are no waves on the Long Island Sound), and watching my boyfriend and Dave Hollingsworth struggle to get a kite sail into the air.

'Hottie alert,' Sidney, stretched out beside me, said in a desultory voice, as a yacht-club waiter staggered by through the hot sand, holding a tray of drinks for some rowdy young moms sitting under a beach umbrella while they watched their kids build sandcastles.

I barely lifted my head. Sid was right. I really do need to work on my tan. Compared to her, I look positively cadaverous.

Sidney was also right about spending the day at the beach. It was gorgeous out – seventy-five degrees with a cool breeze coming in off the water, a cloudless sky, and achingly hot sun. The Sound sparkled in front of us like a blue-green sapphire. We wouldn't have many days like this left. School would start in a couple of weeks, and then it would all be over. Our last summer break before we all left for college.

It helped that Seth, when he'd seen me in my bikini, had purred approvingly, 'Hey, hot stuff.'

Oh, yeah. I'm all about the beach today. Who cares what Tommy Sullivan was doing at Duckpin Lanes last night? Who cares why he was asking about me? He was probably just in town to visit his grandparents after all. He was probably asking Liam about me for old times' sake, nothing more. I mean, why *else* would he be asking about me?

'I'm *over* the waiters here,' I said, in response to Sidney's hottie alert. 'Did you hear about that guy Travis? He was giving *real* Coke to everyone who ordered Diet. Shaniqua told me he was bragging about it down at the Sea Grape. That's so wrong.'

'Not the waiter, doofus,' Sidney said. 'That hottie over there.'

I turned my head to look where she was pointing. It seemed as if there were guys everywhere – hot ones and some not-so-hot ones – in their baggy swim trunks, struggling to lift windsails or tossing around a football or playing killer frisbee. That's the thing about guys, I've noticed. They are completely incapable of sitting still. Unlike me. I could lie in one position and not move for hours.

If I didn't have to go to the bathroom all the time from all the Diet Coke I kept consuming.

'Not *that* one,' Sidney said, noticing the direction of my gaze. '*That* one, coming out of the water right now. The one with the freestyle board. The *redheaded* one.'

40

My head swivelled around so fast I heard the bones in the back of my neck crack.

It couldn't be. It *couldn't*.

Because the guy coming out of the water was over six foot tall – almost a foot taller than Tommy had been, last time I'd seen him – with a golden tan. The guy coming out of the water was also totally cut. Not in a muscle-bound meathead kind of way, like some of those guys I'd seen over in the weight room at the Y, but with a lean, athletic body, nicely defined biceps, and a set of abs that would have made an actual six-pack jealous.

Whereas Tommy Sullivan, when I had last seen him, had had a sunken chest, skin as white as milk (where it wasn't covered in freckles), hair the colour of a new copper penny and arms as skinny as toothpicks.

Well, OK, I might be exaggerating a *little*. Still, he hadn't exactly been anything much to look at.

Not like this vision before us, who was shaking water out of his slightly overlong reddish-brown hair as he leaned over to lay down his board (revealing, as he did so, the fact that beneath his baggy swim trunks – so weighted down with water that they had sunk somewhat danger-ously low on his hips – lurked what appeared to be an exceptionally well-formed gluteus maximus).

Sidney, who seemed no more capable of tearing her gaze away from this example of a god in human form than I was, said, 'I think I've died and gone to Hottie Heaven.'

'Dude, you've got a boyfriend,' I reminded her auto-matically.

41

'Dude, so have you,' she reminded me back, failing to mention – because she didn't know – that actually I've got *two* boyfriends.

But it was really hard to remember either of them when Windsurf Boy straightened up from setting down his board, turned around, and began to stride towards the clubhouse . . . and us.

Sidney's hand shot out to seize my wrist in a grip that hurt – mostly because she was digging her French manicure into me.

'Dude, he's coming this way,' she breathed.

As if I couldn't see that for myself. Windsurf Boy was moving through the sand directly towards us . . . not quite the most direct path to the clubhouse. I was glad the lenses of my Ray-Bans were polarized, so I was able to take in the fine details that might otherwise have been impossible to see, considering the glare from the water . . . the golden hair coating his legs . . . the sliver of matching hair snaking up that lean, flat belly from the waistband of his swim trunks . . . the square jaw and wide, slightly smiling mouth . . . the laughing amber eyes, squinting in the strong sunlight, because his sunglasses were dangling from a cord around his neck . . .

Wait. *Amber eyes?*

'Hi, Katie,' Tommy Sullivan said to me in a deep voice.

Then he went right on past us, climbing the steps to the clubhouse deck and disappearing through the double doors into the cool, air-conditioned lobby.

42

Four

Sidney turned her incredulous gaze towards me the minute the double doors eased shut behind him.

'Wait a minute,' she said, whipping off her own sunglasses to stare at me. 'You *know* that guy? Who *is* he? I've never seen him before. I'd remember *that*.'

But I couldn't reply. Because I was totally frozen.

Tommy Sullivan. Tommy Sullivan was back in town. Tommy Sullivan was back in town and had said *hi* to me.

Tommy Sullivan was back in town, had said hi to me, and was *hot*.

No. No. This did not compute.

Suddenly I was on my feet. I couldn't lie there a second more. I was freaking, basically.

'Katie?' Sidney shaded her eyes with one hand and peered up at me. 'Are you OK?'

'I'm fine,' I said automatically.

Except that I was lying. (So what else was new?) I wasn't fine. I was far from fine. I needed to get out of there. I needed to . . . I didn't know what I needed. I turned towards the steps to the clubhouse deck, then realized that was totally the wrong place to go. That was where Tommy had just gone!

And I didn't want to run into Tommy.

So I turned around again and headed towards the water.

'Katie?' Sidney called after me. 'Where are you going? You're not going in the *water*, are you?'

I didn't answer her. I *couldn't* answer her. I started walking towards the water, past the kids building sandcastles – one of whom went, 'Hey!' indignantly when I accidentally caused one of his turrets to fall down.

I didn't apologize. I kept walking, past the toddlers playing with their grandmothers at the edge of the sand, past the older kids in the knee-high shallows, past the even more daring kids who were paddling around in water up to my thighs, or floating around on inner tubes.

Behind me, I heard Sidney call, 'Katie!'

But I kept walking, until the water was up to my waist, and then finally my ribs, and then the soft sandy bottom disappeared beneath my feet, and I took a deep breath and squeezed my eyes shut and let myself sink.

It was quiet under the water. Quiet and cold. I thought about staying down there, where Tommy Sullivan would never, ever find me.

But then I remembered about the E. coli, and it occurred to me some of it could have floated up to the private beach. Just because the yacht club keeps the tourists off its beach doesn't mean it can keep their poo out of its water.

So I swam to shore really fast and staggered back to my towel, dripping and cold. But at least I had driven the image of the new and improved Tommy Sullivan from my brain. Instead all I could think about were infectious diseases.

Which, believe me, was preferable.

'What was all *that* about?' Sidney asked me when I collapsed, panting from my swim, on to my towel.

'I just got hot,' was my lame excuse.

'God, I guess,' Sidney said. 'I thought you hated going in the water. I thought it made you sick to be in it.'

'Just on it,' I said. 'Seasick.'

'But you have that other thing, that thing about germs—'

'I'm sure it will be OK today,' I lied. 'It looks clear.'

'Oh. So who was that guy anyway?'

'Um, that guy?' Bacillus. That's what E. coli is. A form of bacillus. That's what I needed to concentrate on. Bacillus. Not Tommy Sullivan. And the fact that he's back. And hot. So hot. 'Oh, that was the guy Liam was talking about last night.'

Which, I thought, impressed with myself, wasn't even a lie.

'The one he knows from football camp?'

'Uh-huh.' Well, OK. *That* was a lie.

'Mmmm,' Sidney said appreciatively. 'Remind me to enrol in football camp sometime.'

And that was it. That was the end of the conversation. Especially since Tommy didn't come back. I lay there – after hitting the outdoor shower for about twenty minutes because of, um, bacillus – waiting, tense with anxiety, frantically wondering what I would say if he came back and tried to talk to me . . .

But he seemed to be gone.

Maybe, I told myself, that hadn't been Tommy after all. Maybe it had been some guy I'd waited on at the restaurant or something. Maybe he'd just *looked* like Tommy Sullivan. Or how Tommy Sullivan would look if he turned hot.

Maybe it was just a coincidence Liam having met a guy named Tommy Sullivan last night and me seeing a guy who looked like he could have been an older, hot Tommy Sullivan today.

Only . . . if he wasn't Tommy Sullivan, how had he known my name?

And what about those amber eyes?

Seth and Dave came in from the water soon after that, and we clambered on to the deck for Cokes. No sign of Tommy Sullivan. Or the Guy Who Could Be Tommy Sullivan If Tommy Sullivan Had Turned Hot.

Maybe it had all been in my imagination. Maybe that guy had been someone we knew from high school, some kid I'd never noticed before who'd grown six inches over the summer and started working out, like my brother or something.

It was possible. Stranger things have happened.

By the time I had changed and pedalled over to the Gulp for work, I had all but forgotten the entire incident at the beach – not to mention Liam's alarming news. Not because I'd been concentrating on thinking about bacillus instead, but because Seth kept telling me how great I looked in my bikini (I knew the bike thing would pay off). He told me what a great year we were going to have – our senior year – and how good we were going to look when we were crowned Prom King and Queen.

Which, I'll admit, is kind of a cheesy thing to say. Seth and I do have actual intellectual conversations from time to time. Well, intellectual might be stretching it. But every once in a while I'll drag Seth to a photography show in the city and try to explain the images to him, why they work or don't work, in my opinion.

And OK, usually we just end up making out in some park or whatever.

But Seth's more like the strong, silent type. He's just a really good person.

Which is why, you know, I can never break up with him. Because that would be mean, and I'm not a mean girl.

Which is why even after the Prom King and Queen remark, one thing led to another, and soon we were making out in the cab of his four by four . . . even though it was broad daylight and I had a six-hour shift looming ahead of me.

It's just very hard to worry about some guy you haven't spoken to in four years when some other guy's tongue is in your mouth. Especially when it happens to be Seth

Turner's tongue, which is probably the most sought-after tongue in all of Eastport. At least, among teenage girls. And some of the boys too.

It wasn't until I got out of Seth's truck and biked to the back of the restaurant, to the employee entrance, that I saw Eric Fluteley waiting for me over by the bike rack.

So of course I had to chastise him for the whole Morgan Castle thing. Which wasn't easy to do while simultaneously making out with him, but I managed. My mom says I've always had an amazing knack for multitasking, which is why I get such good grades while still being able to have a decent social life and all, and that even when I was a little kid I would watch TV, colour, and make a cake in my Easy-Bake Oven all at the same time.

Which isn't so different, if you think about it, from making out with a guy while telling him what a no-good, lying dog he is at the same time.

I think there must be something wrong with me. I mean, why do I need TWO boyfriends to be happy? Sidney seems totally content with just one.

Although truthfully, sometimes I suspect that I'm not all that happy. Not even with *two* boyfriends.

I know, I know. Selfish, right? I mean, most girls would die for ONE boyfriend, and I have TWO and I'm still complaining.

Yeah. There's definitely something wrong with me.

I punched in at the Gull 'n' Gulp precisely as my shift was starting (because I can make out and still keep one eye on my watch), and was soon so busy that I didn't have time

48

to think about the Seth/Eric situation . . . let alone the whole Tommy Sullivan thing. By six, ten of the tables in my section were full, including two eight-tops – a senior-citizen tour bus making its way up the coast. I barely had time to *breathe*. I *definitely* didn't have time to worry about amber-eyed redheads with washboard stomachs and low-slung swim trunks who may or may not be seeking revenge on me for the wrong I'd done them in the eighth grade.

It wasn't until I went to give the tour bus tables' drink orders to Shaniqua (since I'm underage I can only take orders for, not serve, alcoholic beverages, which at the Gull 'n' Gulp are only beer and wine) that Jill breezed by and said, 'Oh, Katie, did that guy find you?'

'What guy?' I asked. It was already seven o'clock and the place was packed – and noisy. Peggy has Wednesdays off, so we were cranking the tunes back in the kitchen and it was hard to hear anything except, at that particular moment, Fall Out Boy.

'The cute redheaded guy who stopped by earlier today to ask what time you work. I told him you'd be here tonight. Who is he, anyway? He was hot. I hope Seth doesn't find out about him! He'd be jealous.' Jill noticed a new crop of tourists trickling in up by the hostess stand and said, 'Oops! Gotta run.'

I stood there, holding my drink order limply in my hand. A cute redheaded guy had stopped by to ask what time I work?

In a flash I was hiding behind the soda station, stabbing Liam's number into my cell.

49

'Yo.' That is the incredibly annoying way Liam has taken to answering the phone now that he's been asked personally by Coach Hayes to try out for the Quahogs.

'Did you tell Tommy Sullivan that I work at the Gull 'n' Gulp?' I demanded.

'Well, hello, sister dear,' Liam said, in a fake voice that I knew instantly meant one of the Tiffanys or Brittanys was around. 'And how are you this fine evening? Doing well, from the sound of it.'

'DID YOU?' I shrieked into the phone.

'Yeah,' Liam said, in his normal voice. 'So?'

'Argh!' I couldn't believe this. Seriously, it was like a nightmare. 'Is there anything you *didn't* tell him about me, Liam? My bra size, for instance?'

'Um,' Liam said. 'Not being acquainted with that piece of information, no, I did not.'

I was so mad, I could have killed him. Really.

'Just tell me one thing,' I said, closing my eyes as I fought for patience. 'Is Tommy . . . is he tall?'

Liam appeared to consider this. 'About as tall as me,' he said after a few seconds' thought.

Which would make him six one or two. The same height as the guy I'd seen on the beach.

'Is his hair kind of longish?'

'Yeah,' Liam said. 'You could say that.'

I was freaking out again.

'Is he cut? I mean, built?'

'It was hard to tell,' Liam said. 'Considering all the

50

cigarette packs he had rolled into his sleeve. Oh, and the leather jacket.'

'Shut up,' I said. 'I'm serious! Is he?'

'I wouldn't want to meet up with him in a dark alley,' Liam said dryly. 'Let's put it that way.'

I couldn't help letting out a bad word in response to this information. Liam made a tsk-tsking sound.

'Now, now,' he said. 'Is that any way for a potential Quahog Princess to talk?'

Furious, I hung up on him before I could say anything worse.

I couldn't believe it. Tommy Sullivan really *was* back in town.

And he really *was* hot now – a fact that had been confirmed by multiple independent sources.

And apparently, he not only knew where I worked, but when as well.

This was not good. This was NOT good at all.

'Katie?' Shaniqua appeared in front of me. She looked worried. 'Are you all right? Your tour bus is wondering where you disappeared to.'

'Right,' I said. I had to snap out of it. I couldn't let him do this to me. I had to be normal. I had to be cool. 'Yeah. Sorry. I need four Bud Lites, two glasses of Merlot, three Cabs and three Pinots for them.'

'No problem,' Shaniqua said, still looking concerned as I tore past her, back into the dining room. 'Oh, and the corner booth's occupied.'

Oh, great. Just what I needed. Seth and his friends had

come by to sit and eat quahog fritters while I spazzed about having a possible confrontation with a now hot Tommy Sullivan. Was this some kind of punishment for two-timing my boyfriend? If so, it wasn't fair. It's not cheating if all you do is kiss. Right?

I grabbed a few menus – a ridiculous gesture, since every Quahog in town already knew the menu by heart and didn't need to look at it – and beat a path towards the corner booth, fuming the whole time about my recent spate of bad luck. A tour bus, Tommy Sullivan back in town, and now my boyfriend and his friends here to watch me wallow in my misfortune. Great.

Except that when I got to the corner booth, Seth and his friends weren't in it. Only one person was in it.

A person with reddish-brown hair, worn on the longish side.

A person who appeared to be, considering the way he was folded a bit uncomfortably behind the booth, quite tall.

A person whose eyes, in the light from the stained-glass-covered undersea fish lamp hanging above the table, were a pure, intense emerald green.

A person who was one hundred per cent most definitely *not* a Quahog, and therefore ineligible for seating in the corner booth, which Jill should have known, except that Jill is in college and doesn't go to Eastport High, and he'd obviously asked for me, so she'd just assumed . . .

I dropped the menus. I didn't mean to. My fingers seemed to go limp, and the menus just slid out of my hands. Feeling my cheeks turn red with mortification as I saw Tommy's gaze go to the floor, where the menus fanned out in every direction, I ducked down to scoop them up. I couldn't even count on my hair to hide my flaming cheeks, since Peggy makes us wear our hair up so it won't get in the food.

Not that it would have mattered if my hair had been down, since, when he leaned out of the booth to help me gather up the menus, Tommy would have seen my glowing face anyway.

It was only when all the menus had been retrieved and I'd straightened up and he'd leaned back into his seat in the booth that I dared lift my gaze to meet his again.

And saw that he was smiling. *Smiling*.

'Hi, Katie,' he said, in the same deep voice he'd used when he'd walked by Sidney and me on the beach. 'Long time no see.'

Five

I said the first thing that popped into my head.

Well, not the first thing, since the first thing was a swear word, and I'm trying really hard not to swear. Except at my brother.

I said the second thing instead:

'You can't sit there.'

And OK, I know it sounds infantile.

But it was the truth.

'Excuse me?' Tommy lifted his eyebrows.

'You can't sit there,' I said again. I knew I sounded childish. But I couldn't help it. My heart was pounding a mile a minute and I felt nauseous, like when I forget to take a Dramamine and go out in Dad's boat. 'This booth is reserved for Quahogs only. And you're not a Quahog.'

Which could, quite possibly, qualify as the understatement of the year.

'I'm aware of that,' Tommy said mildly, in his new – well, probably not so new to him, but new to me – deep voice. 'I may have been away a while, but I'm still passingly familiar with the local customs. I think I'll stay here anyway. Your friend Jill has already assured me all the other tables in your section are full.'

As he said Jill's name, he looked over at the hostess stand. I followed his gaze and saw that Jill was looking at us. She waved at us cheerfully, as if to say to me, 'Look! I did you a solid! I got your hot friend a table! You can thank me later.'

Tommy smiled at her.

Incredibly, Jill, who gets flirted with by about a zillion male customers a day, blushed and looked away, giggling.

Unbelievable.

Well, she didn't know. She didn't know that she was flirting with *Tommy Sullivan*. How could she? She didn't even live here four years ago.

'Tommy,' I said, looking back at him. I couldn't believe this was happening. I couldn't believe I was actually *talking* to him. At the Gull 'n' Gulp of all places.

'It's just Tom now, actually,' he said with a smile.

And I suddenly found myself feeling what Jill must have felt, when he'd directed that smile of his in her direction a moment earlier. Wherever he'd been since I'd last seen him, Tommy – I mean, Tom – Sullivan had taught himself how to smile in a manner that caused some kind of secret electromagnetic force or something to make cartilage in girls' knees melt. I had to grab the edge of the table and hold on just to keep from toppling over.

'Tom, then,' I said, from between gritted teeth. Because with God as my witness, there was no way Tommy Sullivan was going to work his new smile-voodoo on me. 'Whatever. You know if Seth Turner and those guys come in and find you here in their booth, they'll pound your face in.'

'They can try,' Tommy said. Not in a bragging way. But in a matter-of-fact, totally unruffled, almost bored kind of way.

And can I just say that when he said it, my knees went even *more* weak.

Because there's nothing sexier, it turns out, than a guy who isn't scared of your boyfriend pounding his face in.

But the fact that it was *Tommy Sullivan* making me feel this was what was completely freaking me out . . . just like down at the beach earlier. Suddenly, I had this insane desire to wade out into the ocean and dunk my head in it again, E. coli or no. I needed to cool off. I needed to be alone. I needed to be underwater with just the fish and the seaweed.

Only I couldn't. Because I was at work.

'Nobody's forgotten what you did, Tommy,' I heard myself snarl at him. 'I mean, Tom. I know it was four years ago, but this is a small town, and the Quahogs are still pretty much gods around here, so—'

'Wow! They've finally got you drinking the Kool-Aid too, huh?' His tone wasn't accusatory. He actually sounded kind of amused. His eyes – still green as the tail of the stained-glass mermaid in the lampshade above his head – were laughing up at me.

And that just made me madder, for some reason.

'I don't know what you're talking about,' I snapped.

'I mean, you've really been assimilated, haven't you?' He shook his head. 'I can't believe Katie Ellison, of all people, is one of *them* now. I always thought you were smarter than that.'

'There's no *us* and *them*, Tommy,' I informed him. 'There never was. We're all just people.'

'Right.' The laughter in his eyes disappeared. He didn't sound amused any more. 'That's why I got run out of town. And that's why I'm not allowed to sit here.'

Before I could open my mouth to protest – because that's NOT why he wasn't allowed to sit there. He wasn't allowed to sit there because only Quahogs (and their dates) could sit there – I heard Shaniqua calling my name. I turned and saw her signalling me from the twin eight-tops. My tour bus needed attention.

'I gotta go,' I said to Tommy. 'But seriously . . . you can't sit here.'

'Technically,' Tommy said, 'I can. Especially given that I already am.'

'Tommy.' I shook my head. I couldn't believe this was happening. 'What are you doing here? Seriously?'

'Seriously? I just want to talk to you,' he said, dropping the dry tone. 'And from what your brother told me, this is the place I'm most likely to find you without your boyfriend . . . or should I say, *boyfriends*?'

I blanched. Suddenly, I had to grip the table harder than ever.

He knew. He knew about Eric.

Only . . . how? Liam couldn't have told him, because

Liam doesn't know. I know Liam doesn't know, because if Liam knew, he'd have yelled at me about it already, on account of being such a fan of Seth's . . .

So how had Tommy figured it out?

Then it hit me. First the yacht club . . . now this.

'Are you *spying* on me?' I demanded with an outraged gasp.

'Spying implies sneaking around,' Tommy said mildly. 'You're the one who seems to be excelling at that, not me. Although you should probably know, anyone who turns their car around in the parking lot out back has a perfectly clear view of anything going on between the emergency generator and that bike rack.'

Oh my God! *Busted!* Tommy Sullivan had full on busted me making out with Eric Fluteley!

I was sure I was going to pass out. Not that I'd ever passed out before. But this must be what it feels like – a sort of hot feeling all over, with accompanying dry mouth. No wonder people don't like it. Never had I wanted so badly to be someone – or someplace – else. Such as Sidney van der Hoff. Or underwater.

'We can't talk here,' I heard myself murmur.

'Fine,' he said calmly. 'Not here. Where then?'

Good question. Where could we go where neither Seth nor anyone else from Eastport might see us together? Duckpin Lanes was out, for obvious reasons. My house? No way. Ditto Tommy's grandparents'. What if someone drove by and saw us together – a Quahog Princess candidate and *Tommy Sullivan*?

58

Oh God, this was awful. I was going to be sick. I really was. What did he want? What could Tommy Sullivan possibly want from me?

'How about your dad's boat?' Tommy asked. 'Does he still have it?'

My dad's boat? Yes. Yes, that might work. It was tied up down at the bight. My dad couldn't afford the docking fees over at the yacht club. No one goes to the bight, except old men who like to night fish. No one would see us there. No one who mattered, anyway.

'Yeah,' I said. 'Down at the bight.'

'Perfect,' Tommy said. And he actually slid out of the booth. I couldn't believe it, but he seemed to be leaving. He was leaving! It was like a miracle! 'I'll meet you there after your shift. When do you get off? This place closes at ten on week-nights, right?'

My happiness that he was leaving died a quick little death.

'W-wait,' I stammered. 'Tonight? You want me to meet you on my dad's boat *tonight*?'

'Is that going to be a problem?' Tommy asked. Standing, he was so much taller than I was that I had to lift my chin in order to be able to see up into his eyes . . . which, out from under the reflective light of the undersea lampshade, were back to amber-coloured. 'Because if it is, I could probably find time to meet you there tomorrow morning. But, you know, in broad daylight, anyone might drive by and notice us—'

'Tonight's fine,' I said quickly. 'I'll meet you there as soon as I go off shift. A little after ten.'

The edges of his lips curled upwards. 'Don't be late,' he said.

And then he was leaving, looking impossibly tall and broad-shouldered and cool amid all the chubby, pasty-legged tourists waddling around us on their way to the bathroom or the hostess desk or the Gull 'n' Gulp merchandise counter, where you can buy anything from a sweatshirt to a pair of boxer shorts, all emblazoned with the words *Gull 'n' Gulp*.

'Who's the hottie?' Shaniqua came over to ask as I continued to stand there gaping after him.

I closed my mouth, which I realized had been hanging open, with a snap.

'Nobody,' I said.

'Right,' Shaniqua said with an evil laugh. 'Like that guy last night – the one Peggy said she caught you making out with behind the soda station – was nobody?'

So much for Peggy not liking gossip. Apparently, gossip is fine – if she's the one dishing it out.

'Not like that guy,' I said quickly. 'Nothing like that guy. Do you even know who that was?'

'Last night? Or this one?'

'This one.' I had to tell someone. I just had to. I was going to burst if I didn't tell someone.

And who better to tell than Shaniqua, who didn't even grow up in Eastport, and only moved here two years ago

60

from New Hampshire in order to live closer to the city, where she's trying to break into the modelling business?

'That was Tommy Sullivan,' I said to Shaniqua, even though I knew the name would mean nothing to her.

Except that I was wrong. Because Shaniqua's jaw dropped.

'*The* Tommy Sullivan?' Her eyes were wide.

'Um,' I said.

'Miss.' One of the seniors from the tour bus was trying to get my attention. 'Miss, we're ready to order now.'

'Be right there,' I said to him. To Shaniqua, I said, 'Wait . . . *you*'ve heard of Tommy Sullivan?' Seriously, this whole thing had got WAY out of proportion if even aspiring models from New Hampshire had heard of Tommy . . .

'Heard of him?' Shaniqua shook her head. 'How could I not have? All you have to do is drive past the middle school and there it is, spray-painted right on the outside of the gymnasium wall: *Tommy Sullivan is a—*'

I cut her off before she could say it. 'Yeah. I know. They're still trying to raise the money to sandblast it off.'

'Is that why it's still there?' Shaniqua shook her head. 'I always wondered. They could paint over it . . .'

'You can't really paint over Day-Glo orange,' I said. 'I mean, unless you use black. And that's not one of the school colours.'

Shaniqua wrinkled her nose. 'Well, it sure looks tacky. I heard that gym was brand new too, when it happened. How could someone do something so stupid?'

I shrugged, suddenly feeling as if instead of being

61

underwater in the ocean, the ocean was inside me – cold and vast and very, very lonely. 'You know how kids can be.'

'That poor guy,' Shaniqua said, gazing after Tommy's departing backside. Which, may I just say, was every bit as good-looking as his front side. 'What'd he do to have something like that spray-painted about him on the side of the school?'

'Miss!' cried the old folks at my tour-bus tables.

'Um,' I said as I started towards them. Saved by the tourists. That was a first. 'Duty calls!'

OK.

OK, so I'm in trouble. Big, big trouble. Tommy Sullivan knows about me and Eric Fluteley. Tommy Sullivan – *Tommy Sullivan*, of all people – saw me with Eric Fluteley.

And OK, whatever, we were just kissing. That's all I've ever done with any guy, including my steady boyfriend of almost four years.

But that won't matter if Tommy spills the beans. People won't care. I will still be the girl who cheated on a Quahog. Not just any Quahog, but Seth Turner, the brother of Jake Turner, the most beloved Quahog of all time . . . the very same Quahog whose promising career was cut so brutally short by none other than . . .

. . . Tommy Sullivan.

'Katie, I hope it was OK that I put that guy in the cor-ner booth,' Jill said on her way to seat a middle-aged couple at a two-top by the water. 'I asked him if he was a Quahog and he said he was.'

I had to laugh at that – albeit sarcastically. I mean,

Tommy may be out to ruin my life to get me back for ruining his.

But at least he's still got his sense of humour.

'Yeah, Jill,' I said. 'Not so much.'

'Seriously?' Jill looked stunned. 'But he's so cute. I just assumed . . . he told me he goes to Eastport.'

What? Nice. Good to know I'm not the only liar in town for a change.

'Jill,' I said. 'That guy moved away from here four years ago.'

'Wow!' Jill said. 'Well, I won't seat him in the VIP booth again, if he ever comes back.'

Wait . . . what was I doing?

'Oh no,' I said. 'If he comes back, you can *totally* seat him in the VIP booth.' Because if Seth and those guys ever catch him there, they'll pound him, and my problems will be solved . . .

No. That's just wrong. I couldn't count on my boyfriend to get me out of this one. I got myself into it, and I was going to have to get myself out.

Which meant, first and foremost, calling Seth at my earliest opportunity and telling him not to come meet me after work for our usual make-out session before I pedal home.

'Are you sure, babe?' Seth sounded concerned. And why wouldn't he, since I'd told him that the reason I couldn't meet him was that I thought I was coming down with a mild case of E. coli?

'Totally,' I said into the phone, trying to sound like

someone suffering from a bacillus in their blood system. 'I don't want you to catch it from me.'

Except, of course, E. coli can only be contracted through contaminated food or water. But Seth isn't exactly in AP Bio, like I am. Which isn't to say he's dumb. His talents just lie in regions other than the academic.

'So let's just take a rain check on tonight,' I said. I was crouched behind the soda station, so Kevin, the assistant manager – who, in the way of all assistant managers, was an even bigger tyrant than Peggy, the actual manager – wouldn't catch me on the phone while not on a break. 'I'll probably be better tomorrow.'

'Really?' Seth sounded a bit happier. 'I thought E. coli was like super serious. I thought you had to go to the hospital for it and stuff.'

'Oh no,' I said. 'Not the twenty-four hour kind.'

OK, so whatever. I'm not the only liar in town. But I am definitely the biggest. Seriously, has there ever been a bigger liar than me in the history of Eastport?

Still, at least I feel bad about it. I detected no hint of remorse in Tommy for lying to Jill that he goes to Eastport High. Whereas I really do always feel terrible every time I lie to Seth.

Fifteen minutes after I punched out from the Gulp, I pulled up to the marina on my bike and looked out at the near-empty parking lot, with the boat masts sticking up out of the water beyond it. I stood there in the still evening, looking at the moths that flew up, attracted by the white light from my bike lamp, and listening to the lap of the

64

water. It was hard to figure out which car was Tommy's. I could only see a few beat-up trucks – but those seemed to belong to the old men clustered with their fishing poles below the bridge of the overpass, beneath which striped bass were rumoured to congregate at night.

There was one red Jeep Wrangler, but that seemed like way too cool a car for Tommy Sullivan. It had to belong to some Summer People, who'd docked their yacht in the bight for repairs, or barnacle scraping or something.

But when I pedalled towards the pier, I didn't see any yachts, just the usual cluster of working boats belonging to actual local fishermen and lobster-men. My dad's twin-engined speedboat, with its brown sun-screen – which Dad had been meaning for years to replace and was now a bit on the tattered, faded side – was bobbing up and down at the far end of the pier.

And there was, I could see by the combined light from the half-full moon and the lamps along the dock, someone lying casually across the bow.

Someone who was most definitely not my dad.

I felt something when I saw him. I don't even know what it was. It was like a fireball of emotions shooting through me, including but not limited to rage, remorse, guilt and indignation.

Most of the rage was directed at myself. Because as I pedalled closer to the boat – bikes aren't allowed on the pier but, whatever, there was no one around to stop me – and saw how comfortable Tommy had gone ahead and made himself, lying there on his back, looking up at the stars, I couldn't help thinking how incredibly good he looked in that snug-fitting black tee and those faded jeans that seemed to hug every contour of his lean body.

And those are not the kind of thoughts any girl with a boyfriend should have about another guy. Let alone a girl with *two* boyfriends.

Let alone thoughts she should be having about *Tommy Sullivan*.

Oh yeah. I was in *serious* trouble.

Six

'Hey,' Tommy said when he finally noticed me up on the pier, looking down at him. He leaned up on his elbows. 'Come aboard.'

'No way,' I said.

He laughed. Not in a mean way though. But like he found something genuinely funny.

'Right,' he said, sitting up and swinging his legs down off the bow so they were dangling in front of the door to the cabin below. 'I forgot how much you hate boats. Even ones that are docked. Still get seasick?'

'Just tell me what you want,' I said, clutching the handlebars of my bike and trying to keep my voice steady. 'So I can leave already.'

'Nuh-uh,' he said with a quick shake of his head. 'Take one of those pills you always have with you and climb in.' Even in the moonlight, I could tell his smile was bitter. 'You're not getting out of this *that* easily.'

I felt a burst of rage so pure and intense it nearly knocked me off my bike and into the water below. Which I actually wouldn't have minded. Anything to keep my mind off the fact that Tommy Sullivan was hot now.

Which I couldn't believe I was thinking about. I mean, this guy was practically blackmailing me into associating with him and I *still* thought he was hot?

There's something wrong with me. Seriously.

At least I wasn't the only one. That there was something wrong with.

Because there had to be something wrong with someone who remembered such a mundane fact as that I never go anywhere without Dramamine (non-drowsy formula) somewhere on my person.

And, true, it's tough to live in a seaside town when you suffer from chronic seasickness. I can't even set foot on the *Run Aground* – a boat so tightly lashed to the pier that it barely moves, and a seaside breakfast spot that's incredibly popular with people like my mother, who love anything cute and nautically themed – without thinking I might hurl.

But how had Tommy Sullivan managed to remember this, after all these years?

Scowling, I climbed down from my bike, lowered the kickstand, pulled off my bicycle helmet, and reached into my backpack – into which I'd crammed my still-wet swimsuit from The Point and my make-up and stuff – and pulled out one of the little yellow pills I've carried around habitually since the age of twelve. I tossed it back without even thinking about reaching for the water bottle I also had in my bag. When you've taken as many motion-sickness pills as I have, you don't need liquid to swallow them any more.

Then, still scowling, I swung myself on to my dad's boat – years of long practice (everyone in Eastport has a dad who fishes) had made me an expert at climbing in and out of boats – and felt my stomach lurch, as it always did, when the deck rolled a little beneath my feet. It takes a while for the Dramamine to kick in.

'All right,' I said, dropping my bag and bike helmet on to the deck, then lowering myself on to the padded bench across from where Tommy was sitting. I was trying to maintain a very businesslike demeanour. Because that's all this was. A business meeting. Tommy Sullivan wanted something. And I was going to do my best to provide whatever it was, so that he didn't rat me out to my boyfriend about my other boyfriend. 'I'm here. Now what do you want?'

'I told you,' Tommy said, looking down at me from his perch on the bow. 'I just want to talk.'

'Talk,' I echoed doubtfully.

'Talk,' he repeated. 'You do remember, don't you, that we used to talk quite a bit?'

'That was a long time ago,' I said. I found that it wasn't very easy to meet his gaze – even though that is an important part of maintaining a businesslike demeanour. I know because I occasionally browse through my parents' favourite trade publication, *Realtor Magazine*, and it said so.

But *Realtor Magazine* had never had any articles on how the heck you're supposed to maintain eye contact with a guy whose irises change colours in different lights, and who furthermore looks so good in a pair of jeans that all thoughts of your boyfriend(s) flee at the sight of him.

Seth Turner, I said firmly to myself. You are the girl-friend of Seth Turner, the most popular guy in all Eastport, besides his big brother. Seth Turner, the guy you had such a crush on all through middle school and who you were so happy to snag the summer before your freshman year, when he finally looked your way. And OK, maybe he DID turn out to be a sort of boring conversationalist, but you don't want to break up with him, because what would people think? It is bad enough you are cheating on him with Eric Fluteley. Do not make things even worse.

Except, well, the moonlight was kind of throwing the planes of Tommy's face into high relief, making him look even handsomer and more mysterious than he had at the beach, when I hadn't realized who he was.

And the sound of the water lapping against the side of the boat was way romantic.

God, what is *wrong* with me? I'm worse than Ado Annie, that girl in the musical *Oklahoma!*, who gets so carried away, whatever guy she's with, that she can't say no.

Oh, God!

'So Liam tells me you're running for Quahog Princess,' Tommy said, casually breaking in on my thoughts about kissing him.

Quahog Princess! Yes! Concentrate on that. Anything but Tommy Sullivan's lips.

'Yeah,' I said. 'I am.'

70

Then, because I remembered all too clearly having made fun of Quahog Princesses back when Tommy and I used to hang out together, I added quickly, 'The money's really good. Fifteen hundred bucks for first. Which Sidney will win, of course, but I have a chance at second. The only other candidates are Morgan Castle, and you know she barely even talks. And then there's Jenna Hicks . . .' My voice trailed off. I didn't want to say anything bad about Jenna, who is probably a really nice person. She just never speaks to anyone, so it's hard to tell.

I needn't have worried. Tommy said it for me. He'd always had a way of saying what I was thinking but didn't want to say for fear of seeming mean and becoming as unpopular as he always was.

'Jenna still only wear black?' Tommy wanted to know.

'Yeah,' I said. I couldn't believe he remembered. I mean, it was one thing to remember about me and the Dramamine, considering how much Tommy and I used to hang out together. But it was quite another to remember Jenna Hicks, with whom I was fairly certain Tommy had never hung out. I mean, even Jenna, uncool as she'd always been, had considered Tommy even more uncool than she was. 'Her mom is making her enter. I guess she thinks Jenna'll make some new friends or something. Ones who aren't into, you know. Death.'

Not that it was working.

'Still,' I added. 'Second place is a thousand dollars.'

Tommy whistled. 'That's some scratch.'

'That's what I was thinking. I really want to get the new digital Leica—'

'Still doing the photography thing,' he said. It wasn't a question.

'Yeah,' I said, pushing away a sudden onslaught of memories of all the times he and I had done stories together for the *Eastport Middle School Eagle*, him writing them, me doing the photography – and spending the whole time praying fervently that Sidney didn't find out how much I actually enjoyed being with someone as fatally uncool as Tommy. Probably it was better, under the circumstances, not to think about that.

Still, I couldn't help asking, because I was curious, 'How about you? Still writing?'

'You're looking at the former editor-in-chief,' he said, 'of Hoyt Hall Military Academy's weekly paper, *The Masthead*.'

'No way!' I cried, forgetting how weird this whole thing was in my excitement for him. I mean, editor-in-chief . . . that's big. 'That's so great, Tommy! Editor-in-chief?'

Then I thought of something, and my grin faded. 'Wait . . . did you say *former* editor-in-chief?'

He nodded. 'I resigned. Something better came along.'

'What could be better than editor-in-chief?' I asked wonderingly. Then, because it had just hit me, I cried, 'Wait . . . *military academy*?'

He shrugged again. 'No big.' Then – I guess because of my expression, which was still dismayed – he added, 'I didn't hate it, Katie. I mean, it wasn't like in the movies. For one thing, it was co-ed. Thank God.'

I blinked. I'd forgotten, in those few moments, all about hating him. Instead, I just felt really, really bad.

Although who I felt worse for – him or me – was debatable.

'Oh, Tommy,' I said. '*That's* where you went after . . . here? *Military* school?'

'I *wanted* to,' he assured me with a laugh. 'I thought I could use some self-defence tips. After what happened back here and all, before I left.'

So that was what he'd meant when he'd said, back at the restaurant, *They can try*.

Also why he was so cut.

'I'm surprised you ever came back at all,' I said, staring down at my shoes . . . my Pumas, because it's tough being on your feet all night in flip-flops. 'I mean . . . you have to hate it here.'

'Eastport?' Tommy sounded amused. 'I don't hate Eastport. I love Eastport.'

'How can you say that?' I asked, looking up in surprise. 'After what those guys did to you?'

'You can love a place while still hating certain things about it,' Tommy said. 'You should know all about that.'

I blinked at him. 'What are you talking about?'

'Well, look at you. You're running for Quahog Princess, but you can't stand quahogs.'

I gasped – though secretly I was relieved all he'd turned

out to be referring to was my hatred of quahogs, the bivalve.

'I don't hate quahogs any more,' I lied quickly, climbing to my feet.

'Oh, right,' Tommy said with a sarcastic laugh. 'You wouldn't touch a quahog with a ten-foot pole! You always said they tasted like rubber.'

'They're an acquired taste,' I lied some more, annoyed because he was right – quahogs *do* taste like rubber to me. I don't understand how anybody can stand them, let alone host a town fair in appreciation for them. 'And I finally acquired it,' I lied further. Really, it is amazing what a string of lies I can work up when properly motivated.

'Sure you did,' Tommy said sarcastically, uncrossing his arms – causing me to notice, as he did so, how large his hands had got since I'd last seen him. Our hands used to be exactly the same size.

Now his looked as if they'd be capable of swallowing mine whole.

I dragged my gaze from his hands – wondering, as I did so, why I couldn't stop thinking about how those big hands would feel on my waist, if Tommy Sullivan should happen to reach out and grab me and drag me towards him and start kissing me . . .

Not that he'd given me any indication that kissing was on the agenda. It was just that with the moonlight and the sound of the water and the fact that he'd got so hot and the fact that I'm basically addicted to kissing, it was sort of hard not to think about it.

Tommy apparently wasn't having any problem resisting these kind of thoughts. At least, if his next question was any indication.

'So. Seth Turner. I guess that finally worked out for you too.'

I knew what he meant. I knew *exactly* what he meant. Because Tommy had been one of the few people I'd let in on the secret of my crush on Seth, way back in sixth grade. I'd figured telling Tommy had been safe enough, considering he had no friends but me. So who would he tell?

'Yes,' I said primly. Where was he going with this, anyway?

'He must be an acquired taste too,' Tommy observed.

'You don't know him,' I said, reaching up to tuck a stray curl of hair behind my ear. Because Sidney and I had read in *Glamour* that guys like girls who play with their hair.

Although what I was doing, trying to make Tommy Sullivan like me – you know, *that* way – I don't think I could have explained in a million years.

'Well, well, well,' Tommy said. He didn't seem to notice my hair-tucking thing.

Which – I know! I was totally flirting with Tommy Sullivan! *Tommy Sullivan*, the most hated person in all of Eastport.

But I couldn't help it.

'Things *have* changed since I've been gone,' Tommy went on. 'Especially you.'

'Oh,' I said, uncomfortably aware of just how wrong he was. 'I'm not so different than I used to be.'

'Maybe not on the inside,' Tommy said. 'But on the out-side? You've done the whole clichéd caterpillar-to-butterfly thing.'

Which, you know, was kind of funny, seeing as how he was one to talk.

'I just got my braces off,' I said. 'And got highlights, and learned how to scrunch my hair.'

'Don't be modest,' Tommy said, almost like he was impatient with me. 'It's not just how you look, either. You seem to have miraculously avoided all stigma from having associated with me all those years ago. In fact, from what I've observed, you're one of the best-liked, most popular girls in town.'

'Besides Sidney,' I pointed out, observing that his eyes, in the moonlight, looked neither green nor amber, but almost silver. Also that his lips were very manly and strong-looking.

Who would have thought skinny Tommy Sullivan would grow up to have such nice-looking lips? Not me. That's for sure.

'Sidney's always been popular,' Tommy agreed. 'But not as universally liked as you seem to be. You've got the whole package – pretty, friendly, hard-working, kind to the eld-erly –' I wondered how he could possibly know that, then remembered my tour bus – 'talented, top of the class – now that I'm not around any more to give you some competi-tion – daughter of two well-liked locals, sister to a future Quahog. In fact, except for your apparent inability to stick to just one guy at a time, you've turned out to be perfect Quahog Princess material.'

I'd got so carried away, hearing all the nice things he was saying about me, that I'd swayed as little closer to him so I could hear him better. But when he got to the part about my inability to stick to just one guy at a time, I glared at him and cried, 'Hey! That's not fair! I can't help it if guys are attracted to me.'

'You could probably help making out with them behind the emergency generator,' Tommy pointed out dryly.

I scowled.

'I don't know what you want from me, Tommy,' I snapped. 'But I'm not sticking around a second longer if you're just going to insult me.'

And I whirled around to go.

And just as I'd hoped he would, he reached out and grabbed one of my arms, right above the elbow, and dragged me back towards him.

'Not so fast,' he said with a laugh. 'I'm not through talking to you.'

'Oh, you're through, all right,' I assured him, peeking up at him from beneath my eyelashes (another *Glamour* tip). 'You've done nothing since you got back to town but spy on me and then insult me to my face. You'd better not have come back here to write some horrible exposé about Eastport or something, Tommy, or I swear I'll—'

'You'll do what?' he asked, still sounding amused. 'Drop me like a hot potato and pretend you never knew me, let alone used to come over to my house after school to do our

Scholastic Reading Counts quizzes together and eat my mom's homemade peanut-butter cookies? Oh, wait. You already did that.'

I didn't care what he was saying, though. Because he still had hold of my arm. His hand was so big, his fingers and thumb almost met around it.

And, now that I was standing so close to him, I could smell the faint scent of his aftershave.

It's hard to stay mad at any guy who smells good.

'Well,' I said in a slightly warmer voice. 'If you're not writing some horrible exposé about Eastport, what *do* you want with me then?'

'I just wanted to tell you something,' Tommy said, looking down into my eyes. 'I've enrolled at Eastport High,' he said. 'I'll be going there this fall.'

Seven

'*WHAT?*'

I yanked my arm from his grasp.

'Wait a minute . . . when you said *former* editor-in-chief did you mean . . . Tommy, are you back in Eastport *permanently?*'

'Yes,' he said calmly.

'That's what Jill meant,' I said, starting to pace the length of my dad's boat (thirty feet, bow to stern), 'when she said you told her you went to Eastport High. Because you *do* go to Eastport!'

'I enrolled last week,' Tommy said matter-of-factly.

'Tommy!' This was horrible. This was terrible. This was the worst thing I had ever heard in my life. 'You – you can't do this.'

'Uh, I beg your pardon, Katie, but yes, I can. It's a free country.'

'That's not what I mean,' I said. My chest felt tight.

'If you're upset my attendance is going to cause you to lose your ranking at the top of the class,' Tommy said mildly, 'I guess I can see your chagrin. But I never knew you were *that* competitive—'

'That's not it!' I cried. Because I hadn't even thought of that. It was true that Tommy and I had always competed for first in our class – especially for points in Scholastic Reading Counts . . . and that since he'd left, I'd held the position with ease, not so much because I'm smarter than my peers (the way I always suspected Tommy was), but because I'm one of the few people in our grade who ever actually studies. Because I sort of like it . . . a fact my friends accept, though it seems to puzzle them.

'What I mean,' I went on, 'is that *they're going to kill you.*'

'I thought there was no us and them,' Tommy pointed out. 'I thought we were all just humans. Or is that not what you told me earlier this evening?'

'*Tommy!*' I couldn't believe he was throwing my own words back at me. Also that he was making a joke out of it. 'This is serious! Don't you understand? This is . . . this is . . .' I couldn't think of a word strong enough to project my feelings on the matter. He's the writer, after all, not me. I finally settled for: 'Tommy, this is *suicide!*'

'Your faith,' Tommy said, getting down off the bow and straightening to his full height, 'in my ability to protect myself from your friends is really flattering, Katie.'

I stared at him. I couldn't believe he could be so stupid. But so . . . so . . . hot.

What had happened to him? Tommy Sullivan had never been stupid.

80

Then again, I suppose people *do* change. Tommy Sullivan had never been hot either. And now look at him.

Well, enough is enough, I decided. And I stalked up to him, tilting my chin so I could look him full in the face.

'I am not joking, Tommy,' I said. 'If you think anybody's forgotten what you did, you are sorely mistaken.'

'No,' Tommy said tensely, 'I can see they haven't even bothered to scrape my name off the gymnasium wall yet . . .'

Oh my God. Was *everyone* going to bring that up today? 'Because sandblasting isn't in the budget—'

'No,' Tommy interrupted me tersely. 'Because they *want* people to remember. It's a warning to anyone else who might want to interfere with the almighty Quahogs—'

'Shh!' I said, looking around to make sure the fishermen beneath the bypass hadn't heard.

'Look at you,' Tommy said with a laugh. 'You're afraid even to say anything negative about them out loud.'

'No I'm not,' I insisted. 'It's just that you know how people here are about the Quahogs.' I couldn't help letting out a frustrated groan. 'Tommy, why do you always have to go around *antagonizing* everyone? Don't you know you get a lot further in life by being friendly?'

'That's a funny way to put it,' Tommy said with a smile.

I eyed him suspiciously. 'What do you mean?'

'Well, what you call being friendly I call lying. Like how you're still pretending to have a crush on your boyfriend, even though you're clearly so bored by him you've taken up with another guy –'

I inhaled to deny this, but he went on, 'But I suppose

81

you think it would *antagonize* too many people if you did the right thing and just broke up with him.'

'That—' I started to cry, but he cut me off.

'The thing is, telling the *truth* can antagonize people. But I'm willing to take the heat. Unlike some people.'

'But there are some things people don't NEED to know,' I cried. I couldn't believe that after all this time he still hadn't realized this.

'Like that their two-time first-team All-State defensive end and a number of his teammates cheated on their SATs?' Tommy asked pointedly.

And there it was.

He'd said it. Not me.

It was amazing. All the pain and anxiety from that day four years ago came rushing back, as if absolutely no time at all had passed since then. Suddenly, I was thirteen years old again, in braces and with a wicked case of the frizzies (I hadn't met Marty yet, or learned about product and scrunching), begging Tommy not to do what he was so bound and determined to do, no matter what the consequences.

And the consequences turned out to be far more severe than even I could have foreseen – for both of us.

'I told you not to run that story,' I reminded him, four years after the fact.

'Yes,' Tommy said, leaning back against the door to the cabin and folding his arms across his chest – an act which caused his impressively rounded biceps to bulge a little . . .

a sight from which I resolutely turned my gaze, since it made me feel just a tiny bit breathless, 'you did.'

'It wasn't that I thought it was wrong for those guys to get busted for what they did,' I went on, trying to make him understand something that, four years ago, I hadn't quite understood myself. 'But I still don't see why YOU had to be the person to bust them for it. You could have gone straight to the editor-in-chief over at the *Gazette*. He'd have run it. Mr Gatch has never been in Coach Hayes's pocket like the sports editor.'

Tommy's expression, in the moonlight, could only be described as incredulous.

'It was *my* story, Katie,' he said. '*I* wanted to be the one to write it.'

'But *why?*' I demanded. 'When you had to know how people were going to react?'

'You know why,' he said. 'You know how I felt about sports . . . and the Quahogs in particular.'

'Right,' I said. 'Which is why I don't get why—'

'Because what they did was wrong, Katie,' Tommy explained patiently, like I was still thirteen years old. 'They were tarnishing the team. I mean, who were those guys hurting with what they did? Other students, that's who. Students who were taking the SATs that day and weren't cheating, students who actually studied. And OK, I wasn't one of those students, since I wasn't exactly applying to colleges in the eighth grade. But still. What they did was wrong. And it wasn't like I didn't give them the chance to come forward before I ran it.'

'Oh, right,' I said, rolling my eyes. 'Like they were going to do that. Scholarships were at stake, Tommy! Besides, they didn't think you'd have the guts to really do it.'

'*Scholarships?*' Tommy laughed sarcastically. 'Yeah, that was what everyone was so upset about. That they lost their chance at getting decent scholarships. Come on, Katie. No one cared about those guys' futures. The only thing that mattered to everyone in this stupid town was one thing and one thing only: the state championship.'

'Which they had to forfeit,' I reminded him.

'As well they should,' Tommy said firmly. 'They were a bunch of cheats. They didn't deserve to play.'

'Tommy.' I shook my head. I couldn't believe, after all this time, he still couldn't see the magnitude of what he'd done. 'They were *Quahogs*. I *told* you not to run that article. I *told* you people weren't going to like—'

He held up a single hand to stop the flow of my words. 'Don't worry, I heard you the first time. And I don't blame you, Katie, for choosing to dissociate yourself from me back then. You did what you had to do in order to survive. This is Quahog Country. I understand that.'

He didn't know. I couldn't believe it, but it was true. Tommy Sullivan had no idea *how* I'd managed to pull myself up from the quagmire of unpopularity into which I'd been afraid I'd sink because of my association with him after his story came out in the *Eagle* . . . what I'd done to convince my friends – and more importantly, Seth Turner – that Tommy Sullivan and I were far from chums.

He couldn't know or he'd have said something.

So of course he didn't blame me.

Did he have any idea how many nights I'd lain awake, berating *myself* over and over for what I'd done . . . or *hadn't* done, to be more precise?

Well, I wasn't about to tell him. I mean, it's true I'm a liar, and that, yeah, I'm fairly boy crazy – a pretty much deadly combination.

But I'm not stupid.

'If you know that,' I said, 'then why on earth do you want to come back here, Tommy?'

He smiled. It was a nice smile – the kind of smile I remembered seeing on his face back when we'd both moved up to tenth-grade reading level on our Scholastic Reading Counts lists even though we were still in sixth grade.

'That's for me to know,' he said, still smiling, 'and you to find out. Maybe.'

I stared at him. I did not like the sound of that. I did not like the sound of that one bit.

'You can't possibly think,' I sputtered, trying one last time to convince him how foolish he was being – because, truthfully, I wasn't at all sure I was going to be able to stand it if that gorgeous face of his got smashed in, 'that you can just waltz into Eastport High next week and be welcomed with open arms.'

'Oh, I don't know,' Tommy said breezily. 'All the guys I got in trouble are long gone by now.'

'But their siblings aren't,' I reminded him. 'Like Seth.'

'You really think Seth remembers how it went down?' Tommy asked.

'Of *course* he remembers, Tommy,' I said.

'I wouldn't be so sure,' Tommy said. 'Am I the only one who recalls that Seth Turner used to think trees give off cold air, because when you stand in the shade it's cooler than in the sun?'

I'd felt myself flushing with embarrassment. It's true Seth isn't the brightest bulb in the garden, but . . .

'That was the fifth grade!' I cried.

'My point exactly,' Tommy said. 'By fifth grade, you and I pretty much knew that cold air came from fronts out of Canada. Seth, Sidney, and the rest of them? Not so much. But I guess you'd know better. They were always your friends. Though I gotta say – I think poor, dumb Seth deserves better treatment. Because, really, Katie. *Eric Fluteley?* That guy's no better than the rest of them. He's got hairspray where his brain should be.'

'Oh, like you're so great,' I cried dramatically. Because of course I felt guilty. I knew perfectly well that Tommy was right. I *was* taking advantage of Seth's trusting, inno-cent nature. And I felt rotten about it. Really. 'Going around, *spying* on people—'

'Observing the world around me,' Tommy corrected me. 'It's what a good journalist does. So. Am I to take it from your reaction to all this that you too will be one of the people giving me the cold shoulder in the halls of Eastport High next week?'

I narrowed my eyes at him. 'That depends. Are you

going to give me the same deal you gave Jake Turner and those guys, and let *me* be the one to break the news to Seth about Eric and me, before you do it?'

'Katie.' He looked mockly offended. 'I'm a nark, it's true. But only when it's for the common good. Your sneaking around with Eric Fluteley behind your boyfriend's back hurts no one but your boyfriend – and possibly Eric. It's entirely your business.'

I nearly sagged with relief. 'Oh,' I said. 'Good.'

I was about to say that no, of course I wouldn't be one of the people giving him the cold shoulder in the halls of Eastport High . . . that I would do everything I possibly could to help him try to assimilate . . . when he went on, as if I hadn't even said anything:

'Of course, I do think you might want to ask yourself *why* it is that you can't seem to be satisfied with just one guy. Or even with two, if all that hair twirling and looking up at me from underneath your eyelashes means what I think it means.'

I gaped up at him in total shock. No. No *way*. Had he just . . . had he just implied – more than implied, flat out stated – that I'd been *flirting* with him?

Flushing beet red – with anger, I told myself. Not embarrassment. Because I hadn't been flirting with him. I *hadn't* . . . much – I took a step backwards, away from him, preparing to head back towards the pier, away from Tommy Sullivan and those bright silver eyes of his. That's how NOT interested in flirting with Tommy Sullivan I was.

I couldn't believe he had the gall even to hint that I might have been doing any such thing.

Well, I'd show him. I'd leave my dad's boat without another word. And as for not giving him the cold shoulder next week in the halls of Eastport High, well, no *way* was I going to give him the satisfaction of being friendly. Since he was obviously the kind of person who mistook friendliness for romantic overtures.

Except that the first step I took as I backed away from him was on to my bicycle helmet, and I completely lost my balance and would have landed flat on my butt at the bottom of Dad's boat . . .

. . . if Tommy hadn't thrown out his arms and caught me just before I hit the deck.

It was only natural that I flung both of *my* arms around his neck. Not that I thought he was going to drop me – he seemed to have the situation well in hand – but, you know. You can never be too careful.

How long we stood like that – our arms around each other in the moonlight, with the sound of the lapping water in our ears and our gazes locked on one another's – I'll probably never know. Long enough for me to start feeling positively light-headed – although that could have been the Dramamine.

Which is the only explanation I can give for why my own eyes started drifting closed, and my mouth started getting closer and closer to Tommy's, until suddenly he broke the silence between us by whispering, his breath warm on my face, 'Katie.'

'Hmmmm?' I asked.

'Do you think I'm going to kiss you or something?'

'Oh, *Tommy*,' I sighed, and closed my eyes in anticipation of an intense, soul-searing lip lock.

Except that the next thing I knew, Tommy Sullivan had let go of me.

Seriously.

Oh, he didn't drop me or anything. It's just that one minute I was lying in his arms, and the next I was completely vertical and on my own two feet again.

As I blinked up at him in confusion, Tommy said with a wry smile, 'I think you've had enough kissing for one day, Katie. Come on. Let me drive you home.'

Obviously, I was totally insulted. Not to mention completely mortified. What is *wrong* with me?

I had no choice, of course, but to refuse his offer of a ride. Even if I hadn't had my bike with me I'd sooner have *walked* than ridden home with a cretin like Tommy Sullivan.

Except that it was pretty hard to keep thinking of him as a cretin when he insisted on cruising along behind me in his car – the Jeep Wrangler, it turned out – to make sure I got home in one piece. Because, he said, even with lights and a helmet, he didn't think it was safe for me to ride a bike in the dark, what with all the drunk drivers they bust on the Post Road every night.

Which – OK, I'll admit – was totally sweet of him. Even Seth doesn't follow me when I'm on my bike to make sure

I get home all right. And he's my *boyfriend*, not my mortal enemy.

But then Tommy had to blow any warm feelings I might have been harbouring for him by stage-whispering my name when I was halfway across the dew-dampened lawn to the front door after parking my bike.

I didn't want to turn around. I didn't want to speak to – let alone see – him ever again.

But it had been nice of him to follow me home.

So I stopped, then turned.

'What?' I demanded in my least friendly voice.

'There'll be plenty of time for kissing later,' he had the gall to assure me, in a voice that made it clear he was doing everything possible to keep from bursting out laughing.

I was so mad, I practically hurled my bag at his head, wet bathing-suit and all.

'I wouldn't kiss you,' I informed him acidly, not even caring if Mrs Hall, our snoopy neighbour, overheard me, 'if you were the last guy on earth!'

But Tommy didn't even have the sense to be insulted. He just laughed and drove off.

And it was definitely a *mwa ha ha ha* evil laugh and not the *ha ha* kind.

Eight

'Honey, are you feeling all right?' Mom wanted to know after poking her head into my room before she went off to work the next morning.

'Yeah,' I said in some surprise. It's not often my parents ask after my health, which is exemplary, aside from the motion-sickness thing. Usually they're more worried about Liam, who has a tendency towards sports-related injuries. 'Why?'

'Well, honey,' Mom said. 'It's almost nine o'clock in the morning and you're usually up and out the door by now. You have to admit, being in bed at this hour is highly unusual behaviour. For you.'

'Sorry,' I said. 'I was just . . . thinking.'

That my life is officially over.

'Without your iPod on?' Mom smiled. Because I can't think – much less do homework – without listening to music. Preferably loud rock music. 'Heavens, it must be about something serious. You're not even on the phone to Sidney.'

'Yeah,' I said. 'Well, this isn't something I can really talk to Sidney about.'

'Oh,' Mom said. 'I see. What about Seth?'

Oh God. I shook my head quickly. 'No. Not really.'

'Well,' Mom said. I could tell she was totally hesitating – do her parental duty, open a whole can of worms she'd probably be happier not knowing about, and risk possible lateness to work? Or just say *Have a nice day*, and keep moving? She seemed to remember her Dr Phil's *family first: your step-by-step plan for creating a phenomenal family*, and said, 'You know you can always talk to me, don't you, Katie? Is it something to do with –' She lowered her voice, even though Liam was already outside with my dad, tossing around a football before Dad left for work, and couldn't overhear – 'boys?'

'You could say that,' I said miserably. '*A* boy, anyway.'

'Is it Seth?' Mom asked, dropping the smile and looking worried. 'Katie, is he pressuring you to—'

'Oh God, Mom,' I cried with a groan, realizing belatedly what she was getting at. 'I am not having sex with Seth. Or anyone else, for that matter. I don't even *like* Seth enough to . . .'

Oh God. I dropped my pillow over my face. I couldn't believe I'd even said that. Of course I liked Seth. I *loved* Seth.

It's just that . . . well, Tommy sort of had a point: if I loved Seth so much, what the heck was I doing out there behind the emergency generator with Eric Fluteley every day?

God. Tommy's right. I probably do have some kind of psychological inability to stick with one guy at a time.

But why *should* I, when none of the guys I'm going out with is completely . . . well, *right* for me?

'If it's not Seth,' Mom said curiously, 'who is it? You said it had to do with a boy.'

I took the pillow off my face and stared bleakly up at the white ruffled canopy over my bed. 'If I tell you,' I said, 'you'll never believe it.'

'Try me,' Mom said, leaning against my door frame.

I looked at her. 'Tommy Sullivan is back in town.'

She blinked once. Then twice. Then she said, 'Oh,' her lips staying pursed even after all the sound had left them.

'Yeah,' I said. And dropped the pillow back over my face.

'Well, honey,' Mom said after a while. 'That was a long time ago. There's been a lot of water under the bridge since then. I'm sure no one still holds all that stuff from four years ago against him.'

'Uh,' I said from beneath my pillow. 'My boyfriend does.'

'Oh,' Mom said again. 'Well. Yes, but . . . I mean, after all, it *was* wrong of Jake to cheat. Surely even the Turners—'

'Jake – and his parents, along with Seth, Coach Hayes and the rest of the Quahogs, past and present – still insists it was all a conspiracy to force them to forfeit the state championship,' I said, beneath the pillow.

'Honey, take that thing off your face. I can't hear a word you're saying.'

I took the pillow off my face.

93

'You know what,' I said to her. 'Never mind. Forget I brought it up.'

'Now, Katie, be fair,' Mom said, glancing at her watch. 'I want to talk about this. I really do. But it's going to have to be later. Daddy and I have got a showing. But I want to hear more about this Tommy thing. I'll be back later this afternoon—'

'Don't worry about it,' I said. 'I'm fine.'

'Katie, honey, don't—'

'Seriously, Mom,' I insisted. 'It's fine. Forget I brought it up.'

Mom glanced at her watch again, then chewed a little on her lower lip, even though I've told her again and again not to do this as it scrapes off her lipstick.

'OK,' she said. 'But we'll talk about it over dinner tonight—'

'Can't,' I said. 'I've got a Quahog Princess rehearsal, then my shift at the Gulp.'

'Oh, Katie. Can't you cut back on your shifts a little? I feel as if I've barely seen you this summer . . .'

'When school starts,' I said. Providing I live that long. 'I've already had to give up all my shifts this weekend because of Quahog Princess . . .'

'Oh, but, honey—'

'I need the money,' I insisted.

She rolled her eyes. 'The way you go through money. What on earth do you do with it all?'

Oops! Yeah. That's another lie I've been living with, along with all the others. See, I can't really tell Mom and

94

Dad what I'm actually buying with the money I've earned this summer at the Gulp.

That's because they got me a camera at Christmas. And if they knew I'd been putting money down on a new camera, they'd be all, 'What's wrong with the camera we got you for Christmas?'

The truth is, there's nothing technically wrong with the camera Mom and Dad got me for Christmas. It just isn't a professional photographer's camera. How am I going to take professional photos if I don't have a professional camera?

But I don't want to hurt their feelings. They can't help being completely clueless.

'You should see the cute new velvet jackets for the fall from Nanette Lepore,' I said. Which isn't even a lie. Sidney told me Nanette Lepore does have totally cute velvet jackets for the fall.

I just don't happen to be interested in buying one.

Mom rolled her eyes again – which is ironic, coming from a woman who owns six pairs of Manolo Blahniks at five hundred bucks a pop.

'All right, well, we'll talk tomorrow morning then,' Mom said, giving up. 'See you later. Have a good day.'

She closed my bedroom door again, after taking one last curious look at me. I guess she could tell. I mean, that I wasn't quite myself.

Have a good day. Ha! Right. Yeah, I was going to have a good day all right. I mean, what could possibly go wrong? Let's see: Tommy Sullivan, class outcast with whom I'd nevertheless been friendly and whom I cruelly betrayed four years earlier (though he doesn't seem to know it), is back in town, and is not only aware that I think he's hot now, but also caught me cheating on my boyfriend, who happens to be the little brother of the guy whose life Tommy ruined when he exposed his cheating in a middle-school newspaper exposé . . .

Oh yeah. No problems there. Everything's going to be *fine*.

I. Am. So. Screwed.

Especially since, that first part – about Tommy not seeming to know how I'd betrayed him?

I'm not totally sure it's true.

Something tells me Tommy might actually know perfectly well what it is that I did.

And that might be why he's back here in Eastport.

Because what if the reason Tommy's back is that he wants revenge?

And I've managed to hand him the perfect way to get it, on a bright, shiny silver platter: all he has to do is tell Seth about what he saw behind the Gull 'n' Gulp emergency generator, and my life is over.

Because when Seth confronts me about it, I won't be able to lie. I can lie to Seth about having E. coli. And I can lie to Seth and tell him that I love him, when the truth is I'm not so sure that's true (because if I did love him, what am I doing with Eric?).

But I can't lie – to Seth's face – about what Tommy saw. The thing is, I can't even say I blame him. Tommy, I mean. For wanting to even the score. What I did to him – even I can't believe it, sometimes. He has every right to hate me.

And yet, last night, when I'd been in his arms, I could have sworn . . .

Obviously I was wrong though. Especially when it turned out the whole time he'd just been laughing at me.

Tommy's evil laugh was still ringing in my ears when I stumbled downstairs a little while after my chat with my mom. Liam, I saw, was gone. He had probably snagged a ride to the Y with my parents. He was determined to bulk up a few inches more before Quahog try-out. I'd never seen anyone more excited about anything than Liam was about that stupid try-out.

After downing a couple of power bars from the pantry for breakfast, I dragged my bike from the garage, strapped on my helmet and tried to tell myself I was being ridiculous. Tommy Sullivan was not back in Eastport to get even with me. Because if he was, he wouldn't have warned me. Right? He wouldn't have told me he'd seen me with Eric behind the emergency generator. He'd have just snapped a shot of the two of us together and e'd it to Seth.

Or maybe to the entire school.

Oh God. I am so dead.

It was hard to enjoy my ride downtown. I mean, really. How could he? How *could* he have taken advantage of me like that by sweeping me into his arms that way, then *laughing* instead of kissing me? I am no Sidney van der Hoff, it's true. My mom isn't a former model, and Rick Stamford

97

didn't fall in love with me at first sight that very first assembly of our freshman year (only to dump me three years later).

But still. No guy had *ever* laughed instead of kissing me.

Except Tommy Sullivan.

Who there was obviously something very, very wrong with. I mean, besides the part about having been born Tommy Sullivan.

Comforted by this thought, once downtown I locked my bike up to one of the bike racks – designed to look like an old-time hitching post – outside Eastport Old Towne Photo and went inside the red-brick, decoratively shingled shop.

Inside, Mr Bird was, as always, unhappy to see me.

'You again,' he said grumpily. Because grumpy is his way.

'Hi, Mr Bird,' I said, taking off my bike helmet. 'Can I see it?'

'You gonna make a payment?' Mr Bird wanted to know, still sounding grumpy.

'You bet,' I said, opening my backpack and reaching for my wallet. 'I got another fifty right here. Oh, and I need to pick up my prints from last week.'

Mr Bird sighed, then shuffled away from the register, into the back of his shop. A few seconds later he came out carrying an envelope of photographic prints and a camera.

My camera. The one I'd had on layaway forever.

'Here,' Mr Bird said with a grunt, and set the envelope – and the camera – down on the glass case in front of me.

I picked up my camera – or the camera that will one day be mine – very gently and examined it. The Digilux 2, by Leica, was still as gorgeous as the day it had arrived in Mr Bird's shop, just waiting for someone to come along who could appreciate its outstanding optics, meticulous fabrication, and high-grade materials.

Someone like me.

'Hello, baby,' I said to the camera. 'Don't worry, Mommy hasn't forgotten you.'

'Please,' Mr Bird said tiredly, 'don't talk to the camera unless you intend to pay for it in full today.'

'Not today,' I said with a sigh, and put the camera down, then opened the envelope he'd brought out.

'What d'you think?' I asked him as I flipped through the prints he'd made me.

'Give up the sunrises and the seagulls sitting on piers,' he said crankily, 'and you just might make something of yourself.'

'Are you kidding me?' I plucked out a photograph I was particularly proud of, a picture of a pelican sitting on a boat prow, cleaning its feathers. 'This stuff is gold.'

'*This* stuff,' Mr Bird said, tapping the photo behind it, which was a picture I'd snapped just for fun, of Shaniqua and Jill having a quahog-fritter fight one afternoon during a lull, when Peggy had taken the afternoon deposit to the bank, 'is gold.'

'I agree,' said a deep, male voice behind me.

And I couldn't help letting out a groan.

Nine

'This,' I said, sounding almost as cranky as Mr Bird, when I turned around and saw who was standing behind me, 'is too much.'

'What?' Tommy asked innocently. He'd swiped the photos from the envelope in front of me and was flipping rapidly through them. 'He's right. You've got a great eye for capturing people. Pelicans? Not so much.'

'S'what I been tellin' her for years,' Mr Bird agreed. 'Any hack can take a picture of a pelican. Sell it as a postcard for twenty-five cents. Big deal.'

'Whereas this –' Tommy pulled out a picture I'd taken of Liam and my dad tossing a football out on the lawn, my dad's expression intent, Liam looking a little frightened – 'tells an actual story.'

'Are you following me?' I demanded, snatching my photos back from Tommy, and then giving him the evil eye. Which wasn't easy. Giving him the evil eye, I mean.

Because he looked even better today than he had last night, even though he clearly hadn't put much effort into getting dressed. He was just wearing a pair of baggy cargo shorts, flip-flops, and a Billabong slim tee.

Which was even more annoying given that it was essentially what I was wearing as well, minus the baggy part.

And he looked much better in it than I did.

'Wow,' Tommy said. 'You used to be able to take artistic criticism. What happened?'

'You aren't my editor any more,' I snapped, stuffing my photos back in the envelope Mr Bird had given me. 'Now, seriously. Are you so hard up for female companionship that the only way you can get it is to stalk people?'

'What, I can't shop in downtown Eastport if you're in the same five-mile radius or something?' Tommy looked more amused than insulted.

'Right,' I said sarcastically. 'You aren't following me. You just happened to walk into Eastport Old Towne Photo because you needed film.'

'Um, no,' Tommy said. 'I noticed your bike parked outside. I was in the pharmacy next door, picking up a prescription for my grandmother.' He held up a white plastic bag that did indeed have a prescription bottle inside it.

'You think I don't have anything better to do,' he asked, 'than harass you?'

'Well, what am I supposed to think?' I demanded, flushing. 'You show up where I work, you show up here . . .' I looked over at Mr Bird. 'Do you think that constitutes harassment?'

Mr Bird shrugged grumpily. 'What do I know about it?

All I want is my twenty-seven dollars for the prints and whatever you're putting down today on the Digilux.'

Still blushing – what is it about this guy that I can't stop turning red when he's around? – I reached into my back-pack and pulled out my wallet, counted out twenty-seven dollars to pay for my photos, then laid a fifty-dollar bill on top.

'Here,' I said to Mr Bird. 'What's the balance on the Leica?'

Mr Bird took out his little layaway book (he's one of the only merchants left in the historic seaport district who's yet to computerize his business, or even to learn how to use a computer), looked up my page and carefully calculated my new total.

'Four hundred and twenty-eight dollars,' he said. 'And seventeen cents.'

Tommy whistled. 'Four hundred bucks,' he said. 'For a *camera*?'

'Actually, it's a two thousand dollar camera,' Mr Bird said, adding, almost as if he were defending me (but then, seeing as how he was Mr Bird, I knew this wasn't possible), 'She's paid off almost sixteen hundred dollars of it already.'

Tommy shook his head.

'No wonder you're going for Quahog Princess,' he said, almost pityingly.

Something about the way he was looking at me made even *more* blood rush to my face. It was almost like – I don't know – he felt *sorry* for me or something.

Which is ridiculous, because if there's anyone on the

planet Tommy Sullivan should be feeling sorry for, it's Tommy Sullivan.

'Thanks, Mr Bird,' I said, throwing my prints and my wallet into my backpack and zipping it up. 'See you next week.'

Then I headed for the exit, ignoring Tommy, who trailed along behind me.

It wasn't until he sauntered over to where I was unchaining my bike from the ornate iron rack it was locked to that I lost it.

'Seriously, Tommy,' I said, straightening up from where I'd been bending over my combination lock.

'It's Tom now,' he said calmly. He'd slipped a pair of Ray-Bans over his eyes, so I couldn't see what colour they were today. But I was guessing amber.

'Tom. Whatever,' I said. *What do you want from me?*'

He didn't look the slightest bit ruffled by my question. He didn't even bother to answer it. 'What are those prints for? The ones you just picked up?'

'I – I don't know.' The question threw me. We weren't talking about me. We were talking about him. And what a freak he is. *Still* is. 'Are you trying to get me back, for not hanging out with you any more after the whole cheating scandal came out? Is that it?'

'So are you going to have a show?' Tommy wanted to know. 'A photography show? As your talent for the pageant?'

I kept right on staring at him. 'A *show*? What are you talking about? No, I'm not going to have a photography

103

show for my talent. Are you insane? Did you even hear what I said before? What was I supposed to do, Tommy? You were a social pariah.'

He ignored my question about his mental health. Also the part about being a pariah.

'Why not?' he asked, apparently with reference to my having a photography show. 'You should. Those photographs are really good, Katie. Well, the ones with people in them.'

OK. Now this was just too weird. He was giving me *pageant* tips?

'First of all,' I said, bending down to yank my bike chain from the rack, 'since when do you know anything about photography? And second of all, you have to *perform* something at a beauty pageant. You have to sing or dance or something.'

Tommy's eyebrows went up. 'Wait . . . you're singing?'

I glared at him. I can't believe he remembered that I'm tone deaf.

No. Wait. I can, actually. Leave it to Tommy Sullivan to remember every *negative* thing there is to know about me.

'I'm not,' I said. 'I'm playing piano.'

His eyebrows went up even further. 'Oh God. Not "I've Got Rhythm"?'

I couldn't believe it. Truly. I couldn't *believe* he remembered.

'What?' I demanded. 'I've got a lot better at it since eighth grade, you know.'

'I've never understood your obsession with that song,'

Tommy said, shaking his head. 'Especially since you don't have any.'

'Any what?' I asked.

'Rhythm,' he said.

'I do so!' Now I *really* couldn't believe it. 'God, Tommy! And for your information, I did *not* want you to kiss me last night, OK? I already have a boyfriend.'

'Two of them,' Tommy reminded me.

'Exactly. Whatever you think was going on last night . . . well, it wasn't. It was all in your imagination. I mean, don't even flatter yourself.'

'And here comes one of them now,' Tommy said.

'One of what?'

'Your boyfriends.'

I followed his gaze and nearly choked on my own spit. Eric Fluteley was pulling up beside us in his dad's convertible BMW.

'Katie,' he said, when he'd come up alongside the sidewalk where we were standing. 'There you are. I've been calling you all morning. Don't you have your phone on?'

I said my favourite curse word (inside my head though, since Quahog Princesses don't swear) and reached into my bag. My phone was off. As usual.

'Sorry,' I said, pressing the Power button. 'I forgot.'

'Thought so,' Eric said with a friendly smile at Tommy, as if to say, *Isn't she cute?* It was clear he had no idea who Tommy was, even though the three of us had been in many of the same classes in middle school. 'I was wondering if you were going to be around later. I'm having trouble

105

figuring out which of those headshots you took to use with my college apps, and was wondering if you could come over to help me figure it out.'

Which was Eric Fluteley Code for *come over to make out with me while my parents aren't home.*

'Uh,' I said, flushing. Because all this was doing was giving Tommy more ammunition to use against me. Even though he was unfamiliar with Eric Fluteley Code. Still, I figured he wouldn't have any trouble figuring it out, since college apps weren't due for months. 'I can't today, Eric. I've got a Quahog Princess rehearsal.'

'Oh, right,' Eric said, laughing in a very fake way. 'How could I forget? I guess I'll see you there. Morgan Castle asked me to be her escort, you know.'

'I know,' I said flatly. Really, he was enjoying this whole make-Katie-jealous-by-hanging-out-with-Morgan-Castle thing a little too much.

'But you'll be at the Gulp later, won't you?' Eric asked in a way-too-casual voice.

'Uh.' I couldn't believe this was happening. That the guy I was cheating on my boyfriend with was trying to make an appointment for more cheating . . . right in front of Tommy Sullivan. And he didn't even know it. 'Yeah. But. Um.'

To my astonishment, Tommy Sullivan came to my rescue.

'Is this the Z4?' he asked Eric, indicating the car Eric was driving.

'Uh,' Eric said, looking at him. 'Yeah, it is. It's my dad's.

Hey . . . do I know you from somewhere, dude? You look familiar.'

And before I could stop him, Tommy was leaning over the side of Eric's car with his right hand extended. 'Sure you know me, Eric. Tom Sullivan.'

I closed my eyes. I closed them because I was pretty certain a gigantic chasmic void had just opened up beneath my feet and that I was about to be sucked down into it.

Because Eric Fluteley only has the biggest mouth in the entire town (well, except for Sidney). The only reason he hasn't told everyone in Eastport about our extra-curricular activities behind the emergency generator is because I told him if he did, he'd have to pay a professional photographer to do his headshots. And that could run into thousands of dollars.

But when I opened my eyes again a second later, I saw there was no chasmic void before me . . . just the Post Road, Eastport's main drag, with Eric Fluteley in his BMW and Tommy Sullivan standing on the sidewalk next to me.

'*Tommy?*' Eric actually tipped down his sunglasses to get a better look at the guy whose hand he was shaking. '*Sullivan?*'

'It's Tom now, actually,' Tommy said, sounding amused by Eric's stunned tone. 'But yeah. It's me.'

'Holy—' Eric said one of the words I, as a candidate for Quahog Princess, have forbidden myself from using. 'What are you doing back in town, man?'

'He's going to be enrolling at Eastport High next week,'

I said quickly, before Tommy could volunteer the information.

'Really?' The corners of Eric's mouth twitched. You could tell he was totally enjoying this. Eric, being concerned only with Eric, doesn't have any sort of feelings for the Quahogs either way. To him, the whole football thing is just a nuisance that takes people's attention away from him. 'Well, if things get rough and you need a hand, let me know. I took self-defence at the Y this summer to help hone my stage-fighting techniques.'

Seriously. Sometimes I wonder why I even let him kiss me.

Although at least when we're busy making out he can't say anything, as his tongue is otherwise occupied.

'Uh, I think I'll be all right,' Tommy said, obviously trying not to laugh. Because the idea of Eric Fluteley fighting anyone is patently absurd. He'd be so afraid of getting his – admittedly gorgeous – face damaged, he'd be of no practical use.

'Well, you're a braver man than I. I'll give you that,' Eric said with a hearty laugh.

A PT Cruiser pulled up behind Eric's BMW and, because he wasn't moving, honked. Eric looked behind him, then said, 'I better get going. See you at rehearsal, Katie. Nice seeing you again, Tommy. Good luck. You're going to need it.'

'Thanks,' Tommy said as a still grinning Eric cruised away. As soon as he was out of earshot, Tommy turned to me and said, 'Seriously. You actually *like* that guy?'

'He appreciates my skills with a camera,' I insisted. 'Which is more than I can say for a lot of people in this town, who wouldn't know the difference between a head-shot and a seascape.'

'I'm kind of doubting it's your skills with a *camera* he appreciates most,' Tommy said dryly.

Giving him a dirty look, I tugged on my bike helmet and, climbing on to my seat, said, as regally as possible for someone straddling a three-speed, 'For your information, I am *not* that type of girl. I don't know what you *think* you saw behind that emergency generator, but it was only kissing. Something you're not going to be doing any of with me, by the way.'

'You bring up kissing me an awful lot for someone who claims not to be interested in actually doing it,' Tommy said, looking highly amused. '"The lady doth protest too much, methinks."'

Furious, I yanked my bike around so it was facing the opposite direction. I meant to start pedalling away from him without another word. But something made me turn around and ask him angrily, 'Tommy, just tell me what you're doing back here. Is it because you want revenge?'

After which, of course, I could have kicked myself. Because what was he going to say? *Yes, Katie, I'm here to get revenge for that thing you did which you don't know that I know you did, but I do know, and I'm going to take you down for it?*

Of course he wasn't going to admit it. Because then I'd start taking evasive action.

Not surprisingly, he played dumb, raising both his eyebrows and going, 'Revenge? On whom? And for what?'

But for once I managed to keep my mouth shut, and instead of being all 'You know what for', I just pedalled away. Which took a lot of self-control, considering.

I know. I seriously need to just give up men entirely. I wonder if Episcopalians can enter convents?

Ten

Eastport takes its annual quahog festival and town fair very seriously. It draws in thousands of tourists and, therefore, millions of dollars of revenue. I have learned from my experience in the food-service industry that people will pretty much put anything into their mouths if it's been rolled in dough then dropped in a deep-fryer (quahog fritters).

And apparently they'll pretty much buy anything if it has a quaint lighthouse or seagulls painted on it. Better yet if it has the words *Eastport Quahog Festival* printed on it (visors, mugs, T-shirts, even thongs).

Because where else are you going to find a quahog festival? (There's one in Rhode Island, actually. But nobody in Eastport appreciates it when you mention this.)

To that end, the town council cordons off Eastport Park, across from the courthouse, the day before the festival begins, so they can start setting up all the tables that will be serving food during the Taste of Eastport, and the booths that will be selling quahog souvenirs, beer and other assorted tchotchkes.

One of the other good things about riding a bike is that you can pretty much dodge around any kind of barrier set up to keep vehicular traffic out of places. Which is what I did in order to get to the other end of the park, where they'd set up the temporary stage in front an enormous white tent (the tent was there for the pageant contestants to change costumes in, before coming out on to the stage), and which was where the Quahog Princess pageant was being held.

I was way too early for rehearsal, of course. Another thing about riding a bike is that you never have to waste time looking for a parking space. I locked up to a nearby park bench (something I wouldn't have dared to do on a normal day, but since the park was technically closed to the public, I knew there wouldn't be anybody to yell at me for it) and slipped into one of the metal folding chairs that had been set up for the pageant's audience, hoping I'd escaped the notice of Ms Hayes, the pageant director.

Yeah. The Quahog Princess pageant is run by the wife of the coach of the Quahog football team, who is also our school's drama director. Ms Hayes, a former Quahog Princess herself, parlayed her win into a shot at Miss Connecticut and, when she won that, at Miss America. She lost that crown, but she made it into the top five semi-final-ists through her crafty utilization of double-sided tape. She's still definitely the most glamorous woman in Eastport – if by glamorous you mean big hair and pink

Lilly Pulitzer capri pants, of which Ms Hayes is fond. Eric, of course, adores her.

'Well, if it isn't Katherine Ellison,' Ms Hayes screeched when she saw me . . . which, unfortunately, didn't take long. 'You have your camera with you, I assume?'

I had the Sony my parents had given me for Christmas in my backpack. I said, 'Yes, ma'am.'

'Good. I ran into Stan Gatch just now over at the Super Stop and Shop, and he said he'd run photos from today's rehearsal in tomorrow's paper to generate publicity for the event if we get the shots in to him by five. Think you can manage that?'

'Sure,' I said, wondering if Ms Hayes actually remembered I wasn't there to take photos but to be *in* the pageant.

But a second later she proved she did remember, when she barked, 'Well, might as well make yourself useful now. Get up here and help me move this piano, since you're the one who's going to be playing it.'

I dragged myself up on stage and, under Ms Hayes's direction, helped the sound guys – who were there to make sure all the mikes were set up correctly – move the piano to the side of the stage, where it would be out of everyone's way until my number.

'There, that's better,' Ms Hayes said, dusting off her hands like *she'd* been the one doing the hard labour. Only she hadn't been, on account of not wanting to mess up her French manicure. 'Now where are the other girls? Tardiness is *not* an attractive trait for a Quahog Princess.'

'Here I am, Ms Hayes,' Sidney called as she hurried down the aisle between the rows of folding chairs, towards the stage. Morgan Castle – clearly coming from ballet practice, since she was still in pink tights, with her hair in a bun – was following her, lugging a duffel bag, presumably with her street clothes in it. Jenna Hicks – looking flushed and uncomfortable in her many layers of black clothing, given the heat – took up the rear. She had the earbuds to her iPod in, and appeared to be off in her own little world. As usual.

'Oh good,' Ms Hayes said. She was clearly in no mood to waste time. From what I've come to understand from Seth, in this way she's a lot like her husband, Coach Hayes. 'Well, let's get to it.'

The next hour was spent going over our blocking (where we were supposed to stand on stage for the various events). Since the town elders had long ago decided that a bathing-suit competition was way too racy for a family-themed event like a town fair – that sort of thing, they felt, belonged to Miss Hawaiian Tropic contests on South Beach – there were only three events in the Quahog Princess pageant: our introduction; talent portion; and evening gown, which was also when they trotted out the question-and-answer segment.

The introduction part was easy. We just had to stand there on stage while the mistress of ceremonies – Ms Hayes – introduced us. After that, we went off stage and into the tent to change costumes for our talent portion. Since my talent – playing the piano – didn't require a costume change (although Ms Hayes tried to persuade me to wear a red, white and blue sequinned body stocking left over from the parade scene of some long-ago Eastport High production of *The Music Man* – which I categorically refused to do), I got to go first.

Which was fine by me, because then I got my part over with that much faster.

Which Ms Hayes says isn't the true spirit of entertaining, but whatever. I was pretty sure I wasn't the only one who felt this way. Jenna Hicks didn't look too upset that her number was last . . . and not because of the whole saving-the-best-for-last thing, either. She truly did not want to be up on that stage. I was surprised she'd made it to rehearsal at all. But when I asked her, she said she'd had no choice: her mom had dropped her off. Jenna'd rear-ended someone the month before and her own car was still in the garage.

'And if I don't place in this freaking pageant,' Jenna explained, 'my mom won't pay the deductible to get my car fixed.'

'Harsh,' I said, a little shocked. I was kind of glad, hearing this, that my parents take zero interest in my extracurricular activities.

Although I did wonder why Jenna didn't just get a bike. I mean, why are people so dependent on cars anyway? It's not like there's anywhere Jenna goes (comic-book store, Oaken Bucket) that she couldn't just pedal to, if she wanted to. Then she could tell her mom to go ahead and keep the money for the deductible, and quit the pageant.

I felt bad for Jenna though, because, even with no-talking Morgan, there was no way she was going to place in the pageant. Her talent, for one thing, was reciting Denis Leary's monologue from the movie *Demolition Man* – the one about supporting the right to smoke cigars in the non-smoking section and run through town naked covered in green Jell-O – a speech not likely to make her particularly popular with the judges, who tend to favor baton-twirling over orations that praise social anarchy.

And Jenna's answers, when Ms Hayes interrogated her during the question and answer segment of the pageant, bordered on the hostile.

Although I guess I could understand why all she said when Ms Hayes asked, 'Jenna, please tell the audience what you love most about quahogs,' was, 'Because they have a hard protective outer shell . . . like me.'

Ms Hayes hadn't been super receptive to that one.

'Now, Jenna,' she said. 'You can do better than that. You want the audience – and, more importantly, the judges – to warm to you, to root for you. You want them to like you, don't you?'

To which Jenna responded, 'Not particularly,' causing Sidney to let out a snorting sound as she tried not to laugh.

'Miss van der Hoff,' Ms Hayes snapped. 'If you can't control yourself . . .'

'Sorry, ma'am,' Sidney said, still looking as if she was going to crack up any minute.

'Now, Jenna,' Ms Hayes went on. 'You want to win, don't you?'

116

'Yeah,' Jenna said, thinking, no doubt, of her car.

'Well, then. Maybe you could attempt to be a little more *likable*. Let's try a different question. Remember, you could receive any one of these questions tomorrow night – they're randomly chosen by the judges. Jenna, in your opinion, what are some traits you consider important in a Quahog?'

Jenna blinked at her. 'You mean like . . . juiciness?'

Ms Hayes looked to the sky, as if she were asking the Lord for support.

'No, Jenna,' she said. 'I meant the team, not the food. Let's try something else. Something easy. Jenna, how would you define true love?'

Jenna just looked at Ms Hayes like she was crazy.

It's kind of funny that as Ms Hayes was asking this, I saw Seth stroll up under the trees, looking tall and cool and hotter than ever, his dark-blond hair flopping sexily over one eye as he grinned up at me.

And I knew, with a burst of clarity greater than any I had ever experienced in my life, what the definition of true love was. It was as if I'd suddenly hit the autofocus on the camera of my mind. True love was Seth Turner – simple, trusting, loving Seth.

And I was filled with a happy, joyous feeling. Who cared if Tommy Sullivan had come back to town? Who cared if the reason he was there was to get revenge on me for what I'd done to him four years ago? Who cared if he'd caught me making out with Eric Fluteley?

Who cared if every time I looked at him I was

117

consumed with a desire to fling myself at him and run my fingers through his hair and lick his face all over? Everything was going to be all right.

Because I had Seth. Sweet, happy-go-lucky Seth, who even now was straddling a metal folding chair beside Sidney's boyfriend, Dave, and making faces at me from the audience, trying to crack me up during rehearsal.

Except that my burst of clarity was short-lived. Because barely a minute later – Ms Hayes had moved on to Morgan, asking her what she loved most about quahogs, and Morgan was stammering something about quahogs being an important source of protein for the area seagulls – Eric Fluteley came striding down the aisle.

And I was horrified to feel my heart swell with love for *him* too! I mean, he just looked so cute, with his dark, curly hair and button-down shirt turned up at the elbows, and his spotless, neatly pressed khakis and sly wink in my direction.

And I couldn't help but remember how sexy he was as Bender in *The Breakfast Club*, and how hot he'd been as Jud, and how complimentary he always was about what he called my chi, or life force, which he says seems really strong, and that probably we were soulmates in a past life.

How is a girl supposed to *not* kiss a guy who says all that to her?

'Miss Ellison.'

So, OK. Maybe I *don't* know what true love is. Maybe I really do need to take a break from boys, instead of looking up the girl-to-guy ratios at the colleges I'm interested in attending next fall, and basing my decision on where to go on which has the highest number of guys (Rensselaer Polytechnic Institute: seventy-five guys to every twenty-five girls. Which sounds just about right to me. Although I'm not actually sure where Rensselaer Polytechnic Institute is, or if they have a photography course. But with that many guys, who even cares? I'll major in microbiology if I have to).

'Miss Ellison!'

Sidney elbowed me hard, and I realized Ms Hayes was talking to me.

'Yes, ma'am?' I asked as Sidney smirked.

'Your turn, Miss Ellison,' Ms Hayes said stonily. 'Please tell our audience – and our judges – what you love most about quahogs.'

'Oh, that's easy,' I said with the smile Sidney had chosen as my best that night we'd practised our Quahog Princess smiles for hours in her bedroom mirror. 'I love their tender succulence – especially when they're floating in a bowl or cup of the Gull 'n' Gulp's world-famous quahog chowder. Mention my name – Katie Ellison – and get a free cup all weekend!'

Out in the audience, Seth and Dave burst into enthusiastic applause. Even Ms Hayes looked pleased.

'Excellent response, Katie,' she said. 'That's one the judges will love. Did you hear, ladies, how Katie managed to mention her sponsor in her answer?'

'I don't have a sponsor,' Jenna reminded us. 'My mom's paying for this.'

'Which is why your response should have been something along the lines of, *What I love most about quahogs are the hot and tasty quahog cakes my mom makes for me on cold wintry days*,' Ms Hayes said.

'My mom doesn't make quahog cakes,' Jenna said. 'She's too busy with her Pilates workouts.'

Ms Hayes lifted her gaze towards the sky again. Then she said, in measured, even tones, 'I think that's enough for the question-and-answer segment, girls. Let's move on to evening gowns, since I see your escorts are here . . .'

The guys stood up and ambled over to the stage, where we greeted them with enthusiastic embraces. At least, Sidney and I did. Morgan Castle, not being on kissing terms with her escort, apparently, sidled shyly up to him and said, 'Hi,' while staring at her feet in her Aerosole Mary Janes. Jenna, however, stayed where she was, centre stage. It soon became very apparent, even to the sound guys, who were so clueless that they'd thought Sidney's Kelly Clarkson song was country and western, that we were one guy short.

'Miss Hicks,' Ms Hayes said, carefully patting her enormous, bouffant hairdo, which a gentle breeze from the Sound was in danger of collapsing. 'Where is your escort?'

Jenna looked down at the toes of her combat boots (seriously . . . . . . her feet had to be sweating so much. I would *not* want to be there when she pulls those things off). 'I don't have an escort,' she said softly.

'I beg your pardon, Miss Hicks?' Ms Hayes said. 'You have to speak up, honey. I can't hear you if you mumble.'

'I DON'T HAVE AN ESCORT,' Jenna yelled.

Ms Hayes looked astonished. Clearly, from her expression, in the history of the Eastport Quahog Princess pageant there had never before been an entrant who hadn't shown up with an escort.

'Are you saying you don't know *any* young man who would be willing to act as your escort, Miss Hicks?' Ms Hayes demanded.

'No one who would be caught dead doing something this lame,' Jenna mumbled.

'Excuse me, Miss Hicks?' Ms Hayes went from looking astonished to looking irritated in about a second flat. 'What did you just say?'

'I said no, I don't.' Jenna looked like she wanted to die on the spot. I didn't really blame her.

'Well, one of you boys escort her, then,' Ms Hayes said, pointing one of her pink-and-white nails at Seth, Dave, and Eric – who all exchanged panicked glances, as if to say, *Not me, man.* You *do it.*

Ms Hayes, however, doesn't take any more guff from her players – the dramatic kind – than her husband takes from the football kind.

'Eric,' she said flatly. 'You do it.'

'I'd love to, Ms Hayes,' Eric said in his most actor-y voice. 'But I'm Morgan's escort.'

'You can escort Morgan, then come around and escort Jenna after,' Ms Hayes said, clearly not falling for the actor-y thing.

'But that wouldn't really be fair to Morgan, would it?'

Eric asked. And he even had the nerve to put his arm around Morgan's waist, causing her to widen her eyes and smile a little, as if she wasn't sure whether to be flattered or alarmed.

'Oh no,' Morgan said, her pale cheeks getting a little bit of colour in them. 'It's OK, Eric. Really.'

'I don't need an escort,' Jenna declared . . . and this time she didn't mumble. 'I am fully capable of walking across the stage by myself, Ms Hayes.'

'Don't be ridiculous, Jenna,' Ms Hayes said. 'You have to have an escort. It's Quahog Princess tradition. Seth, you do it.'

I felt Seth stiffen beside me. 'Gee,' he said. And I could tell he was smothering a laugh. 'I'd love to, Ms Hayes. But I'm not sure how Katie would feel about that.'

'I'm fine with it,' I said loudly, feeling a flash of annoyance at Seth . . . and Eric too. What was wrong with my boyfriends that they couldn't stand the idea of being seen onstage with a girl who, OK, might not be Eastport High's most popular, but who's still a human being, for God's sake?

Sidney elbowed me as soon as I said it, though. I knew it was because she didn't want Jenna gaining any kind of edge over us and, if she didn't have an escort, so much the better.

And if Eric had to escort both Jenna and Morgan, it basically made both of them look like freaks, paving the way for Sidney and I to take first and second place consecutively . . . not that there had ever been any doubt of this before (at least according to Sidney).

But why was I trying to stir up trouble with my *I'm fine with it*?

Except that I *was* fine with it. What I wasn't so fine with was Seth – and Eric – being so rude about it.

But then something happened that I was so not fine with; it made the other stuff I wasn't fine with seem like nothing.

And that was Eric Fluteley opening his mouth and going, 'Hey, I know. Katie, why don't you call Tommy Sullivan and ask him to escort Jenna, now that he's back in town? I bet he's not doing anything tomorrow night.'

Eleven

Seth didn't drop his arm away from me or anything. At least, not right away.

In fact, *nobody* reacted right away. Everyone just kind of stood there, going, 'What?'

Except for Eric, of course, who was busy laughing at his own joke. Which wasn't even technically a joke, since it wasn't funny. To anyone but him, anyway.

Then Seth looked down at me through those impossibly long lashes of his, and went, 'What's he talking about, babe?'

And suddenly, I knew. I knew just what Tommy Sullivan was doing back in town.

And the memory of how I'd almost let him kiss me – *would* have let him kiss me, if he'd tried. Which he hadn't – caused colour to flood into my cheeks. I hoped no one would notice. Maybe I could just blame it on the heat, if anyone asked.

'Oh, nothing,' I said dismissively. 'I ran into Tommy

Sullivan downtown this morning, and Eric was just driving by.'

'That freak,' Seth said. I knew that if Ms Hayes hadn't been around, Seth would have used a different word to describe Tommy . . . one that also started with the letter F, but wasn't quite as socially acceptable as *freak*.

'Well, his grandparents still live here,' Dave said.

Then, because Sidney glared up at him – I guess because she was wondering how he knew so much about Tommy's grandparents – Dave added defensively, 'What? They go to my church. He's probably here visiting them.'

'No he isn't,' Eric said before I could give him a look to shut him up. 'He's starting at Eastport High next week. Isn't that what he said, Katie?'

I closed my eyes again, expecting that chasm I'd thought was going to split open in front of Eastport Old Towne Photo to appear before me. You could have heard a pin drop in the silence that followed this statement. Or, this being Eastport, a quahog spit, over by the Sound.

Then Seth cried, '*WHAT?*' at the same time Ms Hayes declared, 'Enough with the chitchat, people. We haven't finished our rehearsal.'

I opened my eyes. Still no chasm.

But I really, really wanted to jump into one anyway.

'Seriously,' Eric said, looking slightly alarmed by the decibel level of Seth's outburst . . . which was high. 'He told us so himself. Didn't he, Katie?'

That's when Seth dropped his arm from around my waist.

'Wait a minute,' he said, staring down at me with hurt in those puppy-dog brown eyes of his. 'Tommy Sullivan is back in town? And you didn't *tell* me?'

And there it was. Exactly what Tommy was doing here, confirmed:

HE WAS TRYING TO RUIN MY LIFE.

But no way was I going to let him. Even if I maybe deserved to have my life ruined, for ruining Tommy's, four years earlier. I mean, isn't there a statute of limitations on life ruinage, anyway?

'Honestly, I didn't think it was that big a deal,' I said, blinking up at Seth with my most innocent expression – the one Sidney and I had practised in her bedroom mirror in the event we were ever caught by our boyfriends issuing hottie alerts for other guys. 'I only just found out myself. And, I mean, all that stuff with Tommy was so long ago. I figured it was all just water under the bridge.' (Thanks for that one, Mom.)

But it was clear it wasn't all water under the bridge for Seth.

Which I'd sort of known.

'My brother lost all his scholarships because of what that guy did!' Seth cried.

'I know,' I said. 'But – seriously, Seth – don't you think Tommy's been punished enough for it?'

'Why?' Seth demanded. 'Because someone spray-painted that he's a freak on the middle school's gymnasium wall? You think that's the same thing as what happened to Jake?'

'You guys *did* run him out of town,' Jenna Hicks piped up as she inserted the earbuds to her iPod.

Seth shot her a quick look. 'Tommy Sullivan ran *himself* out of town,' he said.

'Yeah,' Jenna said with a laugh. 'Because you guys were gonna kill him.'

'Hey, now,' Dave, being the smoother-over again, said. 'That's not true.'

Jenna let out another laugh. 'Right,' she said sarcastically. Then she switched on her music so she couldn't hear the conversation any more.

I envied her.

'People!' Ms Hayes clapped her hands sharply. 'That is *enough*! We still have work to do! Take your places . . . and – Miss Hicks. *Miss Hicks!*' Jenna switched off her iPod and looked at Ms Hayes tiredly. 'If you don't show up with an escort tomorrow night, you won't be allowed to participate in the pageant. Do you understand?'

Jenna rolled her eyes. 'Yes, ma'am.'

We all hurried to take our places, guys to one side of the stage, girls to the other. As soon as we were out of earshot of Seth and Dave, Sidney pinched me and hissed, 'Why didn't you tell *me* Tommy Sullivan is back in town? That is *huge!*'

I wanted to whisper back, 'I thought you already knew. You issued a hottie alert for him yesterday at the beach.'

But then I remembered how I'd already lied and

told her that guy was someone Liam knew from football camp.

Seriously, it can get to be a problem when you can't keep all your lies straight any more.

Something Tommy had already apparently realized. And which was no doubt part of his diabolical scheme to ruin me.

So instead I just said, 'I didn't think it was that big a deal.'

'Are you kidding?' Sidney whispered back. 'I wouldn't be surprised if the guys are planning a blanket party for later.'

My stomach lurched. Because a blanket party is what the Quahogs call it when they jump a guy and beat him up (in the old days, they'd put a blanket over the victim's head so he wouldn't know who was hitting him. Now they don't bother, on account of the fact that so many of Eastport's cops are former Quahogs, and Quahogs don't rat out other Quahogs).

'That's barbaric,' Jenna Hicks, who'd overheard, hissed.

'Yeah.' Morgan looked pale, but resolute. 'Violence is never the answer to any situation.'

Sidney looked from them to me, and then burst out laughing – presumably at Jenna's and Morgan's naivety.

I pretended to join in with the laughing. But inwardly I really wasn't seeing anything too funny about the situation. Mostly I just wanted to kill Eric for bringing up Tommy in the first place. What's the matter with Eric

Fluteley anyway? For a guy who claims he wants to go out with me (in public . . . not just make out behind an emergency generator) so badly, he sure had a funny way of trying to win me over.

Then again, Eric didn't know that, just last night, I'd been fighting an urge to stick my tongue in Tommy's mouth.

Or maybe he *did* know – some kind of boyfriend sixth sense – and that's why he was trying so hard to get Tommy killed.

It was hard to concentrate during the rest of the pageant rehearsal. Seth seemed really upset – I could feel his bicep tense up every time I slipped my hand through the crook of his elbow so he could 'guide' me to my spot on the stage . . . and I was pretty sure he wasn't doing it to impress me with the size of his arm muscles either, but because he was super worked up over the Tommy thing.

He didn't mention it to me again though. I really hoped that was because he was coming to grips with the idea of Tommy going to Eastport High, and not because he was plotting what Sidney had mentioned – a blanket party. With Seth, it's always hard to tell, because he's so quiet a lot of the time.

I used to think this was because he was really sensitive and deep.

But lately I've sort of come to realize it's because most of the time, he's just thinking about what he's going to eat next . . . a lot like my brother, Liam.

A lot of guys aren't actually all that deep, it turns out.

Well, except Tommy Sullivan. Who apparently has been carefully plotting my social annihilation for the past four years. It's obvious he's just been waiting until I'd risen to my current level of popularity/happiness before making his move. Because the higher they are, the harder they fall.

And what could be higher than being Seth Turner's girlfriend and Sidney van der Hoff's best friend?

Freakishly, I had played right into his hands with my own weakness where hot guys are concerned. If he hadn't caught me making out with Eric Fluteley, he'd have had nothing on me.

Well, nothing except my desire to make out with him too.

God, what is *wrong* with me?

Rehearsal couldn't end soon enough. The minute the photo op was over – Ms Hayes had me snap shots of Morgan dancing and Sidney pretending to sing – Ms Hayes was like, 'Well, I think that's it for the day, people. Remember, you need to be here no later than six tomorrow night.' I kissed Seth goodbye and took off for my bike, saying I had to get my photos over to Mr Gatch at the *Gazette* in order for him to publish them in tomorrow morning's edition.

After all that emotional trauma (not to mention Ms Hayes), it was a relief to cruise over to the offices of the *Eastport Gazette*. Because whatever crazy thing tends to be going on in my life, it fades in comparison to the crazy things that go on at a small-town newspaper. When I walked in, someone was standing at the classifieds desk screaming about his neighbour's barking dogs and how the paper had to print a story about it or this person was going to take his story to *The New York Times* . . . and then we'd all be sorry.

I swear the entire town of Eastport, Connecticut, is made up of wackadoos.

I downloaded my pageant pictures into the art director's computer. She promised to look them over and forward the best ones to Mr Gatch, who was in a meeting. I thanked her and was on my way out – I had to get home to change before my shift the Gull 'n' Gulp (Peggy won't allow us to wear shorts to work, unless they're neatly pressed white or khaki ones) – when I noticed the person Mr Gatch had been having the meeting with coming out of his office.

And nearly had a coronary.

Because the person was over six foot tall, dressed in cargo shorts and a Billabong slim tee, with broad shoulders and longish, red-brown hair.

He didn't see me. Mostly because I ducked behind a filing cabinet.

I couldn't believe it. *I couldn't believe it.* What was *he* doing here?

As soon as he was gone, I hurried over to Mr Gatch's office door, which was still open, and went, '*What was Tommy Sullivan doing here?*'

Mr Gatch, who is a big brusque man with no patience

131

for anyone, most of all freelance photographers who are still in high school, looked up from his computer monitor in an annoyed way and went, 'I'm sorry. But I fail to see how that is any of your business, Ellison.'

I blinked at him. Mr Gatch has a reputation for crankiness, but this seemed particularly ornery to me. It wasn't like he and I were close.

But he had asked ME, and not Dawn Ferris, the staff's only other freelance photographer (she also works part-time at Office Max), to photograph his great-grandson's second birthday party. I had thought this afforded us a certain level of closeness.

Apparently I had thought wrong.

Flummoxed, I stood there in his office doorway, trying to figure out what to do. I could not – would not – leave the building until I knew why Tommy Sullivan had been in it.

Because, deep down, I was pretty sure I did know. I just needed confirmation to make sure I was right, before springing into action.

Mr Gatch had already turned back to his computer monitor. 'Shouldn't you be at Quahog Queen practice or something?' he asked.

'It's Quahog *Princess*,' I said. He knew perfectly well what the proper royal title was. He had only been reporting about it for the past thirty years . . . maybe even more, if the rumours that he was in his seventies were true.

'And I think you should know,' I went on, despite the

fact that Mr Gatch's fuzzy grey eyebrows were lowered, a sure sign he was concentrating on a particularly complex game of computer solitaire and did not wish to be disturbed. Still, it was as if I were seized by some kind of mania. I *had* to know what Tommy had been doing in his office. I just *had* to.

Which is the only explanation for why I blurted out what I did next. Which was, 'The Quahogs are planning a blanket party for him.'

No sooner were the words out of my mouth than I was desperately wishing them unsaid. What was *wrong* with me? I was ratting out my own boyfriend – well, one of them anyway – to the town's biggest gossip (well, besides my best friend and my other boyfriend).

Mr Gatch's fuzzy grey eyebrows instantly lurched upwards. But not, as I assumed, because he sensed a lead and was trembling with excitement to write it.

'Are they now?' he asked me mildly. 'And just what do you expect *me* to do about it?'

'Well,' I said, flummoxed again. 'I . . . I don't know. I just thought you should know.'

Mr Gatch's hatred for the Quahogs (due to his dislike of all organized sports) was legendary. He was the one who'd spied Tommy's story in the *Eagle*, gone ahead and checked on Jake Turner's SAT score (which had, indeed, gone up by three hundred points from his previous attempt at the exam), and the scores of the other team members Tommy had fingered (equally impressively – and incredibly –

133

spiked), and blew the story townwide (and, ultimately, statewide).

Surely, hearing that the Quahogs were now planning something as dastardly as a blanket party, Mr Gatch would leap to his favourite cub reporter's defence . . . maybe write one of his scathing, bitter editorials, like the one that had outraged so many town officials about how so many cats in town were suffering from hyperthyroidism, a direct result, Mr Gatch believes, of impurities in Eastport's drinking-water supply.

But instead, Mr Gatch said, 'If there's anyone who should know, it would be Tommy Sullivan, don't you think, Katie?'

I stared at him, open-mouthed. Warn *Tommy*? Was that what he was saying? That I ought to warn Tommy what Seth and his friends were planning?

But . . . what would be the point in that? Tommy Sullivan was back in town for one thing and one thing only: revenge. To ruin the lives of everyone who contributed to the ruination of his, four years earlier.

In other words . . . mine.

Surely, it was in my best interests to let Seth and his friends do their worst.

Wasn't it?

And yet . . . if it was, what was I doing in Mr Gatch's office, hoping my telling him what the Quahogs were up to would induce him to stop them, somehow?

There was only one explanation for it. And it wasn't one I liked at all.

Swallowing hard, I said, 'Sorry to have disturbed you, Mr Gatch.'

And then I turned around. And I got out of there as fast as I could.

Twelve

So. It had happened at last. Liam's taunt, with which he'd been teasing me for years, was finally coming true.

I should have realized what was going on a long time ago. It all made perfect sense. The fact that I was going out with the hottest, most popular guy in school . . . yet making out, behind his back, with another guy.

The fact that I couldn't bring myself to decide which of these guys I liked better, because the truth was I didn't like either of them all that much, except to make out with.

The fact that I had lied about it to both of them – and my best friend, and all their friends, and my parents, and myself too – so many times, I couldn't even figure out any more who I'd told what when or about whom.

It had been there all the time, the plain, simple truth. Liam had been the only one ever to accuse me of it to my face:

Liar, liar, pants on fire.

It was true. I am a liar.

I knew Mr Gatch was right, and that I had to tell him.

Tommy, I mean. Even though I was convinced he was up to no good – and the fact that I'd seen him in Mr Gatch's office just proved it. Whatever the two of them were cooking up together, you could bet that nothing good was going to come out of it. At least, nothing good for Katie Ellison.

And yet . . . could I really stand by and let that gorgeous face get bashed in?

No. I couldn't.

Which I will admit makes me insufferably weak. But is that really such a surprise? That I'm weak, I mean? *I make out with guys behind emergency generators*. What else is someone going to call me? Besides a tease, which Sidney already told me I'm in danger of becoming if I don't start putting out. As if I care.

I tried to stop myself though. I took my time about changing clothes when I got home. I checked my email. I flipped through the new *Us Weekly*. I played around with my make-up. I made and ate a tuna-fish sandwich. I waited until the absolute last minute until I had to leave the house or be late for work, then looked up the number to Tommy's grandparents' house, and dialled it.

Tommy's grandmother answered.

'Hi, Mrs Sullivan,' I said, in the chipperest voice I could manage. 'It's Katherine Ellison, Tommy's old friend from school?'

There was a pause, during which, no doubt, Tommy's grandmother thought about the way I had hung her grandson out to dry after he'd done the right thing and stepped forward about what he knew concerning the Quahogs.

Then Mrs Sullivan said, 'Oh, Katie! Hello! How are you? I saw that lovely picture you took of Mrs Hinkley at her great-grandaughter's christening last spring. You are so talented!'

'Um,' I said. 'Thanks, Mrs Sullivan. I'm looking for Tommy. Is he there?'

'Oh, no, dear,' Mrs Sullivan said. 'I'm afraid he's out and about.'

'Oh,' I said. I wasn't sure if I was relieved or disappointed. I told myself I was relieved. 'OK. Well, do you happen to have his cell number? He has a cell, right?'

'Oh yes, he does,' Mrs Sullivan said. 'And he gave me the number . . . let me see. I know it's here somewhere.'

I listened to Mrs Sullivan rustle papers around and then go, 'Bud? Bud, do you know where I put the number to Tommy's cellular phone?'

Then Tommy's grandfather could be heard in the background going, 'I told you to pin it up on the bulletin board. Why don't you ever pin things up on the bulletin board? That's why I hung it there.'

I looked at the kitchen clock. If I didn't leave for work NOW, I'd be late, and Peggy would dock my pay.

'Um, Mrs Sullivan?' I called into the phone. 'Mrs Sullivan, it's OK.'

Mrs Sullivan, after some more rustling, came back to the phone. 'Oh, Katie, dear. I can't seem to find the number.'

'That's OK, Mrs Sullivan,' I said quickly. 'If you could just tell Tommy I called, I'd really appreciate it. All right?'

'All right, dear,' Mrs Sullivan said, still sounding distracted. 'Where *could* I have put that number?'

I hung up, because I had to jet. I nearly got run over about ten times along the Post Road, I disobeyed so many traffic laws trying to get to work on time. I made it, but with only like five minutes to spare.

I was locking my bike up when someone slipped his hands around my waist and whispered, 'Hey there, cutie,' into my hair.

Is it any wonder I whipped around and slapped his hands away? I mean, I was feeling very tense. And I hadn't been having the best day.

'Hey,' Eric said in an offended tone, looking hurt. 'What's wrong?'

'What's wrong?' I exploded. 'What's wrong? *You're* what's wrong, that's what. Why did you have to tell Seth and those guys that Tommy Sullivan is back in town?'

Eric blinked a few times behind the dark lenses of his Armanis. 'What do you mean?'

'What do I mean?' I glared at him. The sun was really bright . . . and hot. I was still panting from my bike ride, and a little sweaty. Which I guess would be one of the advantages of having a car. You wouldn't need to worry about arriving places with pit stains. Still, I stood with my hands on my hips anyway. Because I didn't care if Eric Fluteley saw my pit stains. Not any more. 'Exactly what I said. You were totally trying to stir up trouble.'

139

'I was not!' Eric cried.

'Oh, you so were,' I said. 'What I want to know is, why? What did Tommy Sullivan ever do to you, anyway?'

'Nothing,' Eric said, looking defensive. 'God, what is wrong with you today?'

I stood there, squinting at him in the strong sunlight. What *was* wrong with me today? I didn't even know. Except for the part about me being nuts.

But then again, I'm pretty sure I've *always* been nuts. It's just that this whole thing with Tommy Sullivan finally pushed me to actually admit it to myself.

What was I doing? What was I doing with this guy in front of me, who, yeah, OK, was hot and a talented actor and all?

But was it Eric Fluteley I liked? Or the guys he played on stage? I mean, when I kiss Eric, am I kissing Eric . . . or Bender? Or Jud?

And standing there in the hot sun, listening to the sea-gulls fight over a stray French fry over on the boardwalk, I suddenly knew. It was Jud. Poor, lonely, love-struck Jud. And Bender, who spilt paint on the garage floor. Not Eric Fluteley, with his headshots and his daddy's BMW.

And the realization made me feel a little sick to my stomach.

'You know what, Eric?' I heard myself saying to him. 'I can't do this any more.'

Eric continued to blink behind his sunglasses. 'Can't do what any more?'

'This,' I said, pointing to him, and then to myself.

140

'Whatever *this* is. It's wrong. And I'm not doing it any more.'

Eric's jaw dropped. 'Wait . . . are you *breaking up* with me?'

'Well,' I said. 'No. Since I technically never went out with you. But I'm not going to make out with you any more.'

Eric whipped off his sunglasses and said, 'Katie. You're just dehydrated. I can see that you're sweating. Go inside, have a nice cool drink, and I'll meet you back out here during your break. OK?'

'No,' I said, shaking my head. Miraculously, I didn't feel sick any more. I actually felt kind of good. In fact, I felt like laughing. A little. 'No, Eric, don't bother. I won't come out. It's over. I mean it. I really like you – but just as a friend. OK?'

Eric's expression was incredulous. His ocean-blue eyes were filled with confusion.

'Wait,' he said. 'Is this because I never took you to dinner or something? Because *you* were the one who wouldn't go out with *me*, remember? You kept saying you were afraid people would see us together and Seth would find out—'

'No,' I said. 'It doesn't have anything to do with that, Eric. I just can't do this any more. It's too complicated. And it's not fair to you.'

'I don't mind,' Eric insisted, grabbing for my waist again. But I sidestepped him.

'*I* do,' I said. I knew I needed to turn this around so it

141

was about him and not me, because the only person Eric really cares about is himself, and so that's the only person who actually interests him. So I said, 'You need a *real* girlfriend, one who can devote herself just to you.' The way I should have been devoting myself just to Seth. 'What about Morgan Castle? She really seems to like you. You two have so much in common, with the performance thing. And you guys look really good together.'

That seemed to bring Eric up short. He stopped trying to grab and kiss me – knowing as well as I did, no doubt, that the minute the kissing started, I'd be putty in his hands – and went, 'Really? Do you think so?'

Ha! I knew it would work.

'Totally,' I said. 'Only, you know. You have to treat her right. Because she's a ballerina and all. And they're really sensitive. Kind of like actors.'

He seemed to like this. Well, being an actor and all, he would. Like all actors, he was convinced he was something really special and not just a guy who stands around saying a bunch of stuff someone else wrote.

Then a second later he threw me a suspicious look and went, 'Wait a minute. What's this really about anyway, Katie? Does this have something to do with Tommy Sullivan?'

I stared at him, wide-eyed. 'Tommy? No. Why would it have something to do with Tommy?' Did Eric know something I didn't know? Like what Tommy was up to?

'I don't know,' Eric said, still eyeing me suspiciously.

'Because it seems like everything was going along fine between us until *he* came back to town.'

I wanted to burst out laughing. And not in a happy way either. In a hysterical way. Because what Eric had just said had to be the understatement of the year . . . that everything had seemed to be going along fine until Tommy Sullivan came back to town. Had truer words ever been spoken?

'This has nothing to do with Tommy,' I said.

Except that, as usual, I was lying.

But then I lie all the time anyway. What difference did one more make?

'Well,' Eric said, looking uncertain. No girl had ever broken up with him before in his life. Obviously, he wasn't sure how to act.

Fortunately for me, he chose to be magnanimous about it. I hadn't been too worried he'd go the vindictive route and blab everything about the two of us to Seth. Because Eric values his looks too much and wouldn't want to be the recipient of a blanket party himself.

'If you're sure,' he said to me.

'Oh,' I said. 'I'm sure, all right. Bye, Eric. I'll see you around.'

'Yeah.' He put his sunglasses back on. 'I'll see you at the Quahog Princess pageant. Tomorrow.'

'Tomorrow,' I said with a nod. 'Right. And, um. Thanks.'

It seemed kind of lame to thank a guy for spending so much time kissing behind a restaurant. But what else was

I supposed to say? Quahog Princesses are, above all else, polite.

And Eric didn't seem to mind. He smiled and waved goodbye. Then he sauntered back towards his dad's BMW.

And I dashed inside the Gull 'n' Gulp, punching in with only thirty seconds to spare.

'Cutting it close enough, Ellison?' Peggy wanted to know when she saw me.

'Sorry,' I said. 'Quahog Princess rehearsal ran a little late.' It's amazing how smoothly lies trip off the tongue, once you get used to telling them all the time.

'Right,' Peggy said sarcastically. 'Put your hair up and get out there.'

I scooped my hair into a ponytail and went out into the dining room – where I was greeted by the dozen or so waiting staff, line cooks, busboys and Jill, the hostess, holding a sheet cake shaped like a quahog that had *GOOD LUCK TO OUR OWN QUAHOG PRINCESS* written on it in yellow frosting.

They all – including Peggy, who'd come in behind me – yelled, 'SURPRISE!' at the same time.

I was surprised all right. Especially after the way Peggy had yelled at me. Which she later laughingly confided was just to throw me off the scent of what they'd been planning.

'Ha, ha,' I'd laughed weakly. 'It really worked.'

Still, it was nice of them. I mean, to be so supportive. Well, I guess they're my sponsor, so they have to be.

And since there's always a lull between four o'clock,

when my evening shift begins, and five, when the first dinner customers start arriving, it was kind of fun to sit around, eating cake and looking out at the water.

At least it was fun until Shaniqua, straddling the railing over the water beside me, went, 'So what's the deal with this Tommy Sullivan guy who came in yesterday? Is he really the one who ratted out the Quahogs all those years ago?'

Jill, who was straddling the railing on my other side, sucked frosting off a finger and said, 'Yeah, and how can I get his number? Because that boy is fine.'

I felt a sudden, completely irrational urge to push Jill into the water. Which is weird, because I really like Jill.

Instead of pushing Jill off the railing, I answered Shaniqua's question. 'Yes. Tommy's really the one who ratted out the Quahogs all those years ago. He was covering a game for the middle-school paper, the *Eagle*, and he went into the men's locker room over at the high school to interview some of the players before the game, and overheard them bragging about having cheated off another kid when it turned out the proctor at the place where they were all taking the SATs was a huge Quahog fan and let them get away with it.'

Shaniqua looked disgusted. 'You mean if they hadn't been bragging about it they never would have got caught?'

'Probably not,' I said. 'But, you know. They never thought some little kid from a middle-school paper would rat them out. But Tommy included their quotes about the exam in his article, and Mr Gatch, from over at the *Gazette*, read the article and checked the guys' scores, and . . . well. Coach Hayes was forced to forfeit the state championship, because he lost most of his team.'

Jill flipped around some of her long, shiny blonde hair. 'Wow. That is like tragic.'

'What's tragic about it?' Shaniqua wanted to know. 'Those guys cheated and got what was coming to them. So why was *Tommy* the one who got his name spray-painted across the outside wall of the gym?'

'Well, you know how this town is about the Quahogs,' I said with a shrug, hoping she wouldn't notice how my cheeks had suddenly flamed up.

'Stupid jerks,' Shaniqua said, although the actual noun she used to describe the citizens of Eastport was more colourful than *jerks*. And not appropriate for a potential Quahog Princess to repeat.

And then we all had to get off the railing and come inside, because a bus load of German tourists had just pulled up.

By seven o'clock we were full. Things didn't slow down again until just before eleven, which is when we close on Thursday nights. I was so beat I had to call Seth and tell him not to meet me after work.

And OK, the truth was that the thought of making out with Seth after work in his four by four in the parking lot held about as much appeal as the thought of kissing . . . I don't know. A quahog or something. The bivalve, I mean.

But I really *was* tired. It had been a long day. And I needed to get a good night's sleep, on account of the pageant tomorrow night and all. So it wasn't just an excuse. At least, that's what I told myself.

Still, when I walked out to the rack to unlock my bike after work and heard someone call my name from the parking lot, all the tiredness disappeared from my body.

Because it wasn't Seth's voice.

It wasn't Seth's voice at all.

Thirteen

Seriously. It was like I'd been struck by lightning or chugged a million Red Bulls or something, I was suddenly so wired. All those trays of quahog fritters I'd been hauling around? All those bowls of quahog chowder I'd been handing out? My muscles didn't even feel them any more.

That is hardcore. I mean, that a mere *guy* could make me feel that way. Even when I first started going out with Seth – when I realized that, out of all the girls at Eastport High he actually liked *me* and not any of the Tiffanys and Brittanys he could so easily have had – he had never made me feel that way.

And I have to say I really, really hated Tommy Sullivan for that.

'What do you want?' I turned around to demand in my rudest voice.

Only the words died away a little when I saw how hot he looked, leaning against the front of his Jeep in a circle of light thrown down from the parking lot's single street light. His was the only car left in the lot – everyone else had gone home already. The pier was completely quiet, except for the lap of the water against the retaining wall, and some crickets underneath the emergency generator.

I couldn't help but notice, in the light from the street lamp, that Tommy's arms were folded across his chest in such a way that his biceps were really kind of bulging out beneath the short sleeves of his slim tee.

He had one foot propped back on his front bumper, revealing a hole in the knee of the jeans he'd changed into. I couldn't stop staring at the tanned skin that hole revealed, even though it was just a knee. It was like I was hypnotized or something.

Oh, yes. I hate Tommy Sullivan. *So much.*

'Hey,' he said, unfolding his arms – but not unpropping his foot – when he saw me turn around. 'Thought I'd find you here. What's up? My grandmother said you called.'

I tried to stop myself. I really did.

But the next thing I knew, I was leaving the protection afforded me by the bike rack and emergency generator and walking across the parking lot towards him. It was like I was one of the zillions of moths that were batting around the light from the street lamp above us, drawn not to the glow above our heads, but to whatever it was Tommy Sullivan was giving off.

Which I was starting to suspect was serious pheromones or something. Because how else could I explain why I couldn't seem to stay away from him, despite the fact that he was very obviously back in town in order to destroy me?

'Yeah,' I said, when I'd got close enough to him to see

that his eyes were amber in the light from the street lamp. More yellow than amber, actually. I don't think it was a trick of my imagination. Tommy Sullivan's eyes looked as if they were gold. 'I called you. I . . . I wanted to tell you something.'

'That's what I figured.' Tommy was looking down at me curiously. 'Hey, are you all right? You look kind of . . . funny.'

'I'm fine,' I said, licking my lips. My mouth had just gone really dry. I don't know why. I just kept looking into Tommy's eyes and thinking, They really do look like gold. How is that even possible? How can someone have *golden eyes*?

'Um,' Tommy said. 'Well, you didn't leave your cell number. So I couldn't call you back. I tried your house. But your dad said you were here.'

'Oh,' I said. Tommy, unlike Seth and Eric, didn't wear any jewellery. His neck was unadorned by chains, leather cords, or pooka shells. All he had on was a watch, one of those big-strapped waterproof kinds. I decided that the no-jewellery look suited him.

'So.' He raised his eyebrows. He still looked curious. 'What did you want to tell me?'

What was wrong with me? Why couldn't I stop staring at him? I was acting like one of those stupid love-struck girls who'd been hanging around my brother at the gym. Only without the giggling. Which was ridiculous, because I am *not* in love with Tommy Sullivan. In fact, I hate Tommy Sullivan.

150

Which reminded me.

'What were you doing today in Mr Gatch's office, down at the *Gazette*?' I finally got enough control of myself to ask.

'*That*'s why you called?' Tommy asked, looking incredulous.

'No,' I said. Suddenly, I was blushing. So he wouldn't notice, I pulled out the clip holding up my ponytail, then ducked my head so my curly hair fell over my face. Then I hurried over to lean against the front of his Jeep beside him, so he could only see my profile. 'I just want to know what you were doing there. Is that why you're back in town, Tommy? Because you're writing some kind of story for Mr Gatch?'

'What did Mr Gatch say,' Tommy asked, 'when you asked him?'

I blushed even harder. How had he known?

Except that I knew how. Tommy knew me. Too well.

I kept my gaze on the asphalt, bits of which were sparkling a little in the circle of white light thrown by the street lamp. 'That it was none of my business.'

'Uh-huh.' Tommy folded his arms again. 'And what does that tell you?'

'That it's none of my business,' I said grudgingly.

'Well.' Tommy shrugged. 'There you go then.'

I had forgotten this about him. How frustratingly stubborn he could be. Which is surprising (that I'd forgotten), since it was that stubbornness which had got us into this mess in the first place.

'Tommy,' I said. '*Think* about what you're doing – whatever it is. Don't do anything to make people hate you.'

'How am I supposed to do that?' Tommy asked, laughter in his voice. 'Everybody in Eastport already hates me. What could I possibly do to make them hate me more?'

'I don't know,' I said, turning towards him, not caring any more if he saw my burning cheeks. 'But, Tommy, you should know . . . Eric told everybody about you being back in town, and Seth . . . Seth wasn't happy.'

'I'd imagine he wouldn't be,' Tommy said with a smile that could only be called cynical.

'Tommy, I'm *serious*,' I said, reaching out to lay a hand on one of his folded forearms. Only to make sure he realized *how* serious I was. Not because I wanted to touch him. Not at all. 'Sidney said she wouldn't be surprised if they were planning something. Seth and Dave and the rest of the team. Something like . . . like a blanket party.'

But Tommy, instead of being horrified, just threw back his head and laughed.

I was the one who was horrified. By his reaction.

'Tommy, I don't think Sidney was kidding around!' I cried. 'You need to look out. I think it will be OK, if, like I said, you keep a low profile. But whatever you're doing at the *Gazette* . . . seriously, Tommy. Just stop. Especially if it's going to get them more riled up than they already are.'

'You're too much,' Tommy said when he'd stopped laughing long enough to speak again. He shook his head, grinning down at me. 'You really are.'

'Tommy.' Maybe he didn't understand the gravity of the

152

situation. I laid my other hand on his arm too, and stood to face him, so that I could look up into his eyes – trying not to notice that they appeared to be the colour of the sun – so he'd see I wasn't kidding. 'This is the weekend of the quahog festival . . . the last weekend before school starts up again. You remember what happens this weekend. Right?'

He looked down at my hands a little quizzically. I was also standing pretty close to him. Close enough that my boobs were kind of level with my hands. So maybe it wasn't actually my hands he was looking at.

'Uh,' he said.

'This is the weekend when the Quahogs let off steam before Coach Hayes's practices start for real,' I reminded him. 'Last year all that happened was that a bunch of people lost their mailboxes, because the team went after them with baseball bats out the car window. But this year, Tommy . . . it could be *you* they go after with a baseball bat.'

Tommy's gaze flicked from my chest to my eyes. I wondered if he'd noticed that I'd taken another step closer to him, so that we were now only a very short distance apart. One of my knees was, in fact, rubbing up against one of his.

'Your concern for my welfare,' he said, 'is touching.'

'I mean it, Tommy,' I said. 'I feel bad about . . . well, how things went down between us four years ago.'

'You feel bad,' he repeated. And this time, he was the one who licked his lips.

'Uh-huh,' I said. He had a lot of fine, blond hair on his

arm. I couldn't help stroking it a little with my fingers. 'About how I treated you.'

'Are you sure what you feel bad about is how you treated me?' Tommy wanted to know. His voice still sounded sarcastic. But also a little curious. 'Or is what you feel bad about the fact that I caught you cheating on your boyfriend, and you're afraid I'm going to tell him?'

'You can tell him anything you want,' I said with a shrug. 'Eric and I broke up this afternoon.'

A glance upwards showed me that Tommy had raised his eyebrows in surprise. I looked down again, quickly, keeping my gaze on the silky arm-hairs I was stroking.

'You did?' Tommy's voice wasn't quite as steady as it had been. Still, he hadn't lost one bit of the sarcasm. 'Gosh, I hope it wasn't because of me. I'd hate to know I'd come between you and the guy you're cheating on your boyfriend with.'

Hurt (how could he joke at a time like this, when I was in his arms . . . well, practically?), I dropped my hands from his arm and said stiffly, 'Don't flatter yourself, Tommy. It had nothing to do with you. And you know what? I'm *sorry* I called you today. Or your grandmother. Whatever. Let's just pretend I didn't. I hope Seth and those guys *do* throw a blanket over your head and hit you with a baseball bat. Maybe then you'll finally realize you don't actually know everything.'

And I whirled around to go.

And, just as I was hoping he would, he reached out and caught my wrist.

Only instead of just keeping me from stalking off to my bike, Tommy kind of held on. Next thing I knew, he'd spun me around so I was the one with my back up against the front of his Jeep . . .

. . . and he was the one leaning over me, with his hands resting against the hood, an arm on either side of me, and his face just inches above mine.

'I don't think I know everything,' he said to me in a low voice, his gaze locked on mine with an intensity that was making my heart race. In a pleasant kind of way.

'You don't?' I had no idea what I was saying. All I could think was, He's going to kiss me. I know it. He's going to kiss me, while a detached part of my brain wondered why, if I really hated him as much as I kept telling myself I did, I should be so excited about that.

'No,' Tommy said. He wasn't smiling at all now. There wasn't a hint of humour in his golden eyes. 'Because if I knew everything, I'd have figured out what kind of game you think you're playing right now.'

'I'm not playing,' I protested.

But the word *playing* barely got past my lips before Tommy's mouth came down over mine.

And then Tommy Sullivan was kissing me like I had never been kissed before in my life. Which was ridiculous, because of course I had been kissed hundreds of times before.

But somehow never quite like this, by someone who seemed to feel that he had all the time in the world to get his point across . . . the point being that Tommy Sullivan was kissing me so that I felt his kiss from the top of my head all the way down to the bottoms of my feet, and everywhere in between. He wasn't even touching me – except for his lips, and where his body was leaning up against mine, so that I could feel the Jeep's front grille at my back.

But it was like he didn't *have* to touch me. Every single one of my nerve endings seemed to be on fire. It was like kissing an electrical outlet or something. I felt like I was going to explode.

And I guess Tommy must have felt something along the same lines, because after a minute of carefully not touching me, suddenly his arms went around me, and instead of feeling the front grille of the Jeep behind my back, he'd lifted me so I was sitting on it, and he was kind of between my legs. I'd already flung my arms around his neck. It was all I could do not to wrap my legs around his waist as well.

And all I could think was, Now *this* is a kiss. Seth had never kissed me like this before. Eric neither. It was almost like Tommy had *practised* this kiss or something, that's how good it was.

And as he went on kissing me and I went on kissing him back, it occurred to me that it was really true . . . Tommy Sullivan really *was* a freak.

But like in the best possible way a guy could be.

And then, just as suddenly as he'd started kissing me, Tommy stopped, tearing his mouth away from mine – but not dropping his arms from around me – and looked at me. Because I was perched on the hood of his Jeep, we were at exactly the same eye level, for once. I looked right back at him, my lips feeling delightfully bruised and tingly, my breath coming out a little raggedly.

But not as ragged as his.

'Don't even try to tell me that you learned how to do that in military school,' I said accusingly, when I could speak again.

Tommy laughed. But his voice was as unsteady as mine when he replied, 'I told you. It was co-ed.'

'Oh, yeah.' But this information was hardly comforting. Seriously, Tommy had to have kissed a lot of girls to have got his make-out technique down to such perfection. My head was spinning around so much, I couldn't stop myself from stammering, 'So do you . . . do you have a girlfriend?'

He raised his eyebrows. 'Used to. Why? Would you be more interested in me if I did have a girlfriend, so you could have the fun of trying to steal me away?'

'I'm not like that,' I said hotly, wanting to pull away from him. But then, a stronger part of me wanted to stay right where I was. Forever. 'I don't steal other people's boyfriends.'

'Right,' Tommy said with a laugh. 'You just cheat on your own.'

'I can't help it,' I protested. Although I knew if Seth had ever once kissed me the way Tommy just had, I'd never have looked twice at Eric. Or Tommy.

And then I admitted a terrible thing . . . something I'd never admitted to anyone before. Anyone but myself: 'I just . . . I guess I just don't like him enough not to.'

'I don't think it has anything to do with how much you like or dislike Seth,' Tommy said, absently letting one of the curls of my hair wrap around a finger as he played with it. 'I think it has to do with the fact that you wanted him for so long, and then you got him and you realized he wasn't so great after all. But you couldn't break up with him, because you're Katie Ellison, smartest girl in the class. Breaking up with Seth means you'd be admitting you made a mistake. And brainiac Katie Ellison doesn't make mistakes.'

'Th-that –' I stammered. 'Th-that's ridiculous!'

'Is it? Maybe. Or maybe it's just that you've never been able to stand disappointing people, and if you broke up with Seth that would disappoint a lot of people . . . especially Seth. So you're doing everything you can to get him to break up with you. Only it's not working.'

'Ha!' I cried. 'That's funny! No, really, that's rich. You think I *want* Seth to find out about me and Eric?'

'Exactly,' Tommy said. 'Only he's not bright enough. Really, Katie, the whole thing boils down to how much you dislike yourself.'

I jerked my head away, so the curl fell away from his finger and bobbed back against my face.

'What do you mean?' I demanded hotly. 'I like myself. I totally like myself. *Too much*, maybe,' I added after a second, thinking about Quahog Princess and how sure Sidney and I were that we were going to win.

'I don't think so,' Tommy said, shaking his head. 'I've seen your photos, remember?'

I glared at him in the light from the street lamp. 'What about my photos?'

'You're a great photographer,' Tommy admitted. 'But like Mr Bird said, you're better at taking pictures of other people than you are of anything else. I think because you understand people . . . and you don't judge them. It's *yourself* you don't seem to understand . . . or be totally honest with.'

'What are you talking about?' I shook my head. 'I may lie a lot . . . that's true. But to other people. Not myself.'

'Oh yeah?' He looked amused about something. '*Pelicans*, Katie?'

'So what?' I shrugged. 'So what if I like to take pictures of pelicans? What does that prove?'

'That you're just trying to give people what you think they want. It's not what *you* want.'

Why did I get the feeling he wasn't actually talking about pelicans? The thing was, I didn't know what the heck he *was* talking about. Worse, I didn't even really care. Because all I wanted to do was kiss him some more.

'People like pelicans,' I stammered. Because it was the only thing I could think of to say.

'Yeah,' Tommy said. 'People do. Just like people like quahogs. But *you* don't. People love Seth Turner. But *you* don't. I think the problem with you, Katie, is that you've been so busy for these past few years giving people what you think *they* want, you haven't stopped to think about what *you* want.'

I looked at his lips. I had no idea what he was talking about. I *totally* knew what I wanted. At least, right then.

'Or maybe you have,' Tommy said with a smile, apparently noting the direction of my gaze. 'And it scares you.'

'I'm not scared,' I assured him. And for once I wasn't lying.

And then, much to my satisfaction, he was kissing me again. I'm not at all sure how long we'd have stayed in that parking lot, kissing – or maybe even more than kissing, considering the way things were rapidly seeming to develop – if I hadn't noticed, on the backs of my closed eyelids, a light that was much brighter than the street light we were under.

And then when I opened my eyes, if I hadn't happened to notice the car that had just pulled into the Gull 'n' Gulp's parking lot.

The car with a very surprised-looking Sidney van der Hoff behind the wheel.

Fourteen

My parents were still awake when I got home. Apparently they'd waited up especially for me.

'Hi, honey,' Mom said, lowering the copy of *Realtor Magazine* she was reading in bed, while my dad flipped around the various ESPN channels, looking for the score to the golf game. 'How was your day?'

'Um.' I wasn't exactly sure how to answer that question. Also, I was still in a sort of daze from Tommy Sullivan's kisses. And what had happened right after he'd kissed me. 'Fine.'

Well, what else was I going to say? *Not so good, Mom. I broke up with the guy I've been seeing secretly behind my boyfriend's back and started making out with another guy, one the whole town hates and who I think is trying to ruin my life.*

Only my best friend caught me, so now he doesn't have to bother.

'Sidney called,' my dad said, not taking his gaze from the television screen. 'Twice.'

'Oh,' I said. 'Thanks.'

'Why is she calling on the house phone?' Dad wanted to know. 'Did you forget to charge your cellphone again?'

'Um,' I said. 'Yeah.' No point in telling him the truth – that I'd been sending all Sidney's calls straight to voicemail ever since she'd started phoning, approximately three seconds after she'd bugged out in the parking lot, after seeing Tommy Sullivan and me making out on top of his car.

Seriously, she hadn't even said a word. She'd just thrown her Cabriolet into reverse, then peeled out at top speed.

Then immediately started calling me.

But if Sidney thought I was actually going to pick up, she had another think coming, that was for sure. Not because I'd gone back to making out with Tommy, but because I'd immediately realized the folly of what I'd been doing and had pushed him away, leaped from the hood of his car and raced for my bike.

'Katie,' he'd said, coming after me.

'Go away,' I'd yelled, fumbling with my bike lock. It's hard to work a combination when your fingers are shaking as hard as mine were.

'Katie.' Tommy had leaned against the emergency generator, looking down at me. 'Come on. We've got to talk.'

'No way,' I'd said. I was furious to note my voice was shaking too. What was wrong with me? I mean, I know I like kissing boys and all. But *Tommy Sullivan*? 'Do you have any idea who that was? Any idea at all?'

'It was Sidney van der Hoff,' Tommy said. 'I know, I saw

162

her yesterday on the beach with you over at The Point, remember?'

'Right.' I'd finally got the chain off. 'And in about five seconds flat, the entire town is going to know that I was making out with you in the parking lot at the Gull 'n' Gulp.'

'Well, maybe it's all for the best,' Tommy had had the nerve to say. 'I mean, it's not as if you and Seth were about to win any couple-of-the-year awards, anyway.'

'But I didn't want him to find out *this* way!' I'd raged.

'Maybe Sidney will keep it to herself,' Tommy had said.

'Oh, right! What are you *talking* about? She's Sidney van der Hoff!'

'Yeah, but isn't she your best friend?' Tommy had looked insufferably calm about the whole thing. 'I thought best friends watched each other's backs.'

'She's *Sidney van der Hoff*!' I'd yelled again. Did he not *get* it? We were dead.

Correction: *I* was dead. Nobody was going to think anything about him kissing me. The fact that *I*'d been kissing *him*, though? Everyone was going to hate me. I wouldn't have a single friend left in the whole town.

What a way to start my senior year.

'This is what you wanted all along, wasn't it?' I'd snarled at him as I'd yanked my bike out of the rack. '*This* is why you came back. To get back at me by ruining my life!'

'What?' He'd had the nerve to let out an incredulous laugh. 'Are you serious?'

'Of course I'm serious! And now you're just going to

163

leave, aren't you? You never intended to stick around once you'd done your damage, did you? Don't even try to deny it, Tommy.'

He'd just shaken his head. 'Katie, what are you *talking* about?'

'You *know* what I'm talking about!' I'd jammed my bike helmet on to my head. 'God, I can't believe I was so stupid. I can't believe I let you do that to me!'

'Do *what* to you?' Tommy had demanded, starting to look angry. 'I don't recall doing anything *to* you. You were kissing me back. And pretty enthusiastically, I might add.'

I'd been so furious, I hadn't even been able to reply. I'd just started pedalling. I'd nearly skidded on the gravel going past him, but I'd recovered myself at the last second and torn off, Tommy yelling, 'Katie! Wait!' after me.

I'd thought I was well rid of him. I mean, I pedalled *hard*.

But at the stop sign just before the Post Road, I'd realized he was following me. *Following me*. Ostensibly to make sure I got home all right, the way he had the night before.

But who knows if that had even been his motivation? Maybe he'd just ridden along behind me to make sure what he'd done to me had really sunk in. Maybe he'd just wanted to make sure his humiliation of me was complete.

It had certainly seemed like it when I'd skidded into my driveway and he'd pulled up alongside the yard and actually got out of the Jeep, saying in an impatient voice, 'Katie. This is stupid. You're overreacting. Katie, wait –'

But I'd just dropped the bike – instead of dragging it

into the garage – and gone, 'Leave me alone!' in a voice I hoped was dramatic enough to wake up Mrs Hall next door. Hopefully she'd call the police. Arrest was the least Tommy deserved.

Then I'd run inside the house.

Where I'd found my parents calmly reading and watching television.

'How did the Quahog Princess rehearsal go?' Mom asked brightly.

'Fine,' I said. Was Tommy still outside? Or had he driven away? What did he want from me anyway? I mean, *really*?

And where had he learned to kiss like that?

'Honey,' Mom said curiously. 'Are you all right?'

I tore my gaze from the television screen I'd been staring unseeingly at. 'What? Yeah, I'm fine. I said I was fine.'

'You don't look fine,' Mom said. 'You're flushed. Doesn't she look flushed, Steve?'

My dad looked at me. 'She looks flushed.' Then he looked back at the TV, where Tiger Woods was accepting an award for something.

'I'm not flushed,' I said. 'I'm fine. I'm just tired. I'm going to bed. I have a big day tomorrow.'

'Don't we all,' Mom said, shaking her head. 'You with the pageant, Liam with Quahog try-outs. And Daddy and I have three showings! It's going to be quite a day!'

She had no idea. Especially when news got out about who I'd been macking with in the Gull 'n' Gulp's parking lot.

I just hoped Mom and Dad's business wouldn't suffer. I mean, the real estate bubble has pretty much burst, even in resort towns like Eastport. If word gets out that the only daughter of the owners of Ellison Properties was seen consorting with Tommy Sullivan, their listings would only drop off even more.

Sleep that night was impossible, of course. The one time I really needed it too, in order to look good for the pageant. I just couldn't nod off. I lay there all night, unable to stop thinking about what had just happened. Not even so much the part where I'd seen Sidney's face, looking so surprised behind her steering wheel, either. But the part where I'd made out with Tommy Sullivan.

And I'd liked it.

I'd really, really liked it.

How was such a thing even possible? I mean, Tommy was just the guy against whom I'd always competed in school for top of the class . . . a guy who, because of that competition, eventually became (sort of) a friend. Not a friend I'd ever told my *real* friends (such as Sidney) about. But a friend just the same.

A friend I had horribly, terribly betrayed.

And OK, he'd grown into a total hottie.

But that didn't excuse the fact that I'd basically thrown myself at him.

And yeah, I know there'd been two people in that parking lot. But let's face it, I'd been the only one flirting. And stroking his arm hair? Oh my God, I make myself sick. What is *wrong* with me?

Except that it wasn't entirely my fault. I mean, maybe it was my fault that we'd *started* kissing. But he was the one who kept me wanting to kiss him. He hadn't had to kiss me so . . . satisfactorily. I mean, to the point that I couldn't *stop* kissing him. That was entirely his fault. No guy should kiss a girl like that. Not unless he knows what he's getting himself into.

Which I'm betting the full amount I owe on my Leica that Tommy didn't.

Unless he did. Unless the reason it had seemed as if he'd practised that kiss was because he had. Not like on another girl or a pillow or whatever, but in his mind. Because that's what it had seemed like. That Tommy Sullivan had kissed me like that before, only in his imagination.

But that's crazy. Tommy Sullivan hadn't spent the past four years since I'd last seen him thinking of me. I will admit I have a high opinion of myself, but it's not *that* high.

No, Tommy Sullivan was just a really, really great kisser.

And it's a good thing the only reason he's interested in me is because he wants to get me back for what I did to him in the eighth grade. Because if he was seriously into me, I'd be in big trouble. I mean, he's smart, he's hot, he knows I hate quahogs and he doesn't hold it against me, and he follows along behind me when I ride my bike at night to make sure I get home safe . . . could there be a more perfect guy?

Oh my God. I can't believe I just thought that about *Tommy Sullivan.*

And what was all that stuff he'd said about me being afraid to break up with Seth because I don't like admitting I'd made a mistake? Could any theory be more ridiculous?

And not like myself? *Not like myself?* I LOVE myself! I'm running for Quahog Princess, aren't I?

Obviously, with stuff like that batting around in my head, sleep was impossible. Well, virtually. I guess I must have dozed off at some point, because when I opened my eyes again, bright sunlight was streaming through my windows . . .

. . . and Sidney van der Hoff was standing at the side of my bed, leaning over me and going, 'Katie. Katie. Wake up. Wake *up.*'

I sat bolt upright, got a head rush, and flopped back down with a groan.

'God,' Sidney said, plopping down on to the bed beside me. 'What is the matter with you? You look like total warmed-over quahog casserole. Is that zit cream on your face or . . . oh, it's just toothpaste. God. Bathe much?'

'Sidney.' I longed to smush a pillow over my face. But I couldn't. Because doing so wouldn't make her go away. Or change what was about to happen. 'About last night. What you saw . . .'

'Yeah, really,' Sidney said. She was wearing her stick-straight hair back in a white headband. She had on a freshly pressed white-collared shirt, and jeans with pink sequins sewn along the pockets. On her shoulder was a pink Marc Jacobs hobo bag, and on her feet, pink flip-flops. Since this, for Sidney, was remarkably casual, I wondered where she was going. Or was this just the outfit she picked out for dumping her best friend. 'I called you like fifty million times. Didn't you get any of my messages?'

'I turned my phone off,' I said crankily. 'Who let you in here, anyway?'

'Liam,' Sidney said, looking down at her cuticles. 'On his way to Quahog try-outs. I've never seen anyone so excited. So. Are you going to tell me what that was about last night, or do I have to pry it out of you?'

'Sidney,' I said. How was I going to lie my way out of this one? I really didn't think there was a single way I could work this where I didn't come out looking like a girl who'd cheated on her boyfriend with his mortal enemy.

If you could call kissing cheating, which technically I'm pretty sure in this case it is.

But before I could say anything, Sidney went on, 'I only cruised by the Gulp last night because Dave was at his grandma's and I figured you'd be hanging out with Seth in his truck, and I wanted to see if you guys'd be into grabbing something to eat from the DQ. I didn't think I'd find you *in a liplock with some other guy.*'

I couldn't help it. I grabbed a pillow and smushed it over my face. That was how great my shame was.

Although I'm not sure shame is the right word for it. Because Sidney's use of the word *liplock* brought the memory flooding back of how Tommy's lips had felt on mine. I could feel myself starting to blush. Not because I was embarrassed that she'd caught us, but because of how much I'd really, really liked it.

169

'I'm sorry,' I wailed into the pillow. 'I don't know what came over me! It was like I couldn't help myself! He's just so . . . cute! I mean, you're the one who issued a hottie alert for him!'

To my surprise, Sidney didn't even attempt to deny this. Which is astonishing, since she's way concerned about her street cred, even if the only streets she ever ventures on to are the ones right here in Eastport . . . and Fifth Avenue in the city, of course, but only between 56th (Bendel's) and 50th (Saks).

'Did I harsh on you?' Sidney wanted to know. 'No. I fully understand. But what are you going to do about Seth? He's gonna find out. I mean, this is a small town.'

I wasn't sure I had heard her correctly, so I removed the pillow, just to be sure. 'Wait,' I said. 'Did you just say you *understand*?'

'Of course I do,' Sidney said with a sniff. 'That boy is a fine, fine example of the modern American male. How could you possibly have resisted? I wouldn't have been able to myself.'

My heart warmed. Suddenly I felt more fond of Sidney than I ever had in all the many years of our friendship. It's true she's super judgemental, totally shallow and a huge gossip.

But she can also be the coolest of buds. Like the time I entered that photo contest in *Parade Magazine* and I didn't win, and she took me to Serendipity in the city and split a frozen hot chocolate with me and didn't once point out – as some people might have – that maybe the reason I didn't win was because I don't like or understand myself. Nor did she once mention how many calories we were consuming.

And now this.

'Oh God,' I said, relief coursing through me like cool water after a long bike ride on a hot day. 'Sidney, you have no idea – I can't tell you how worried I've been. I was up all night *freaking out* over what you were going to say—'

'Are you joking?' Sidney looked shocked. 'Why would I care who you make out with in your spare time? To tell you the truth, I'm a little relieved. I mean, it's nice to see you're actually human, for a change.'

I blinked at her. 'What are you talking about?'

'Well, sometimes it's like you're perfect or something.'

Now I was gaping at her. '*What?*'

'Well, it's true. I mean, you're disgustingly good at everything . . . school, the photography thing. Everybody likes you . . . even parents. You don't drink, you don't smoke. You don't even put out. And in spite of that, Seth hasn't dumped you yet.'

I felt a little less warm towards her. 'Gee,' I said. 'Thanks, Sidney.'

She shrugged. 'Whatever. I'm just telling it like I see it. Except for the whole motion-sickness thing, you're like Little Miss Perfect. Although, you know, better not let Seth find out about Mr Football Camp, or he'll flatten the guy's face. And that would just be a waste. Now come on, get up. We've got hair and nail appointments at Spa-By-the-Sea, remember?'

But instead of getting up, I just stared at her. 'Mister . . . what did you call him?'

'What?' Sidney had got up from my bed and gone to look at her reflection in the mirror over my vanity table. 'Mr Football Camp? Isn't that how you met him? You said he's some guy Liam went to football camp with. Oh my God, is that a blackhead? Oh no, just a mascara fleck. Thank God. Hurry *up*, Katie.'

Fifteen

She didn't know. I couldn't believe it. But she really didn't know.

Well, why would she? She'd seen me in the Gull 'n' Gulp parking lot with a guy I'd told her had gone to football camp with my brother. Of course she didn't know that guy was really Tommy Sullivan.

Because the last time Sidney had seen Tommy Sullivan, he'd been a foot shorter and . . . well, not hot. And because I had lied to her about his true identity at the beach the other day.

Once again, I was caught up in a tangle of my own lies.

But that didn't mean I was about to fill Sidney in on the facts of the matter. I mean, I'm not stupid. If she believed the guy she'd seen me with was just some random dude we'd seen at The Point, who was I to disabuse her of that notion? It worked for me.

And, OK, I knew at some point she was going to figure it out. If Tommy hadn't been lying about enrolling at

Eastport High, Sidney was totally going to realize who he really was when school started.

And, yeah, she was going to be mad at me for lying.

But maybe I could get out of it somehow. Maybe I could be like, 'Oh, wait, *that* guy? Oh yeah. That's Tommy Sullivan. I thought you meant that *other* guy . . .'

Yeah. OK. Probably not. I was screwed.

But until Sidney figured it out, I was just going to go with it. Because I had way too much other stuff to worry about than the fact that my best friend thought I would French some guy I barely knew on the hood of his car in a parking lot.

Like, for instance, what I was going to do about Tommy.

Because there was no way I was going to let him get away with this. He couldn't just waltz back into my life and destroy it because of something I'd done to him *four years ago*, when we were both still basically children and couldn't, technically, be held responsible for our actions. Uh-uh. No way. Not going to happen.

Only how was I going to stop him?

That's what I was asking myself as Sidney and I got beautified over at Spa-By-the-Sea (which technically should be called Spa-By-the-Sound because that's what it overlooks. But whatever). Mrs van der Hoff had given us both gift certificates for pre-pageant full-body massages, sunless tanning, non-extraction facials (she didn't want us to be discoloured for the big event), manicures, pedicures, make-up application and hair styling. Which was super nice of her.

It would have been even nicer of Mrs van der Hoff if she hadn't insisted on coming along with us and commenting on everything we did. ('Are you sure you want a French manicure, Sid? You know how tacky they can look if you don't get a thin enough line.' 'Should you really wear your hair down, Katie? It would be so pretty up, with just a few tendrils curling down, here and there.')

Still, it was nice she took an interest. Not that my own mother doesn't. She's just busy with her job – something Sidney's mom, who doesn't work, doesn't have to worry about.

And I have to admit, her presence kept Sidney from asking me uncomfortable questions such as, 'So what's the guy from the parking lot's name?' and, 'When are you going to see him again?' and, 'Does Hottie McHot-A-Lot know you've got a boyfriend? Who's on the football team? And not just any football team, but the *Quahogs*?'

It wasn't because Sidney shied away from embarrassing me in front of her mother. She simply couldn't get a word in edgeways. The only time Sidney's mom stopped talking was when I was under the hairdryer – and that's just because I couldn't hear her with all the hot air blowing around me. I used the opportunity to decide what I was going to do about Tommy. Which was . . . avoid him. I had to. I had no choice. Clearly I couldn't be in his presence and not throw myself at him.

And now that I'd actually tasted the sweet nectar that is Tommy Sullivan's kisses (Ew! But it's true), I knew it was going to be *extra* hard to resist him.

175

But I was just going to have to gird my loins (um, literally) and do it. Because I had *way* too much at stake.

So I would just do everything I possibly could not to be in his presence. If he called my cell, I wouldn't pick up (I don't pick up numbers I don't know anyway). If he called at home, I'd tell whoever picked up to tell him I was in the shower. If I ran into him on the street, I'd turn and go the other way. If I ran into him at the Gull 'n' Gulp, I'd make Shaniqua take his table. If I bumped into him anywhere else, I'd either hide or leave.

I wasn't sure what I was going to do if he ended up in any of my classes at school. Steadfastly ignore him, I guess.

And maybe . . . just maybe . . . if I did all that and word *did* get out that I'd been seen making out with him (because Sidney was going to put it together one of these days. She wasn't *that* stupid), I could just deny it. I could say that Sidney must have inhaled too many fumes from her spray-on nail-polish dryer and was seeing things.

It could work. Just maybe.

Becoming pageant-ready takes a long time. I didn't get home until late afternoon – just an hour before I had to show up at Eastport Park – by which time my brother, Liam, had apparently also just got home from Quahog tryouts. As I walked into the house – my hair up (Mrs van der Hoff won), my tan perfect, my finger and toenails pearly pink and professionally filed, my make-up immaculately applied – Liam was telling Mom and Dad, who were home from the office and sitting at the kitchen counter, listening to him with rapt attention, 'So then Coach Hayes had us do

176

a shuttle run, and I made it in thirty-two seconds, and then he had us do a forty dash, and my time was five point nine metre-seconds, and then we had to run a mile, and I don't know what my time was on that, but it must have been good, because . . .'

That's when everyone finally noticed I had walked into the room, and they turned to me with big smiles on their faces. I knew the smiles weren't because I looked so good. I wasn't even in my pageant dress. Yet.

'Well, hi, honey,' Mom said.

'Katie, Katie, guess what?' Liam could barely contain his excitement.

'Um,' I said, pretending like I had no idea what he was about to say. 'They found asbestos in the school and we're not going to have to go on Monday after all?'

'No,' Liam said. 'I made the junior-varsity team! I'm a Quahog!'

I screamed politely to show my excitement for him, and then the two of us jumped around the kitchen (me being careful not to jump so hard that my hair fell down), while Mom and Dad beamed at us.

'This calls for a celebration!' Dad declared. 'We're all going to Pizza Hut!'

Mom smacked him. 'Steve! You know we can't! Katie has her Quahog Princess pageant tonight!'

'I know,' Dad said, grinning. 'I was kidding. But we could still go after. For a double celebration, when she wins.'

'I won't win,' I said, at the same time Mom said, 'Why

would we go to Pizza Hut when they're having the Taste of Eastport in the park tonight?'

Meanwhile, Liam was going, 'Wow, Katie, if you win tonight then we'll *both* be Quahogs.'

'Yeah,' I said, trying not to think about how quahogs make me gag. 'Great!'

'You should've heard Coach Hayes's speech – you know, to the new junior-varsity team, after all the losers went home—'

'Hey,' I said, not smiling any more. 'They aren't losers just because they didn't make the team. They just didn't make the team.'

'Um, hello,' Liam said sarcastically. 'That is the definition of loser. So Coach Hayes, he goes, "Today is the first day of your new lives . . . not as ordinary citizens of Eastport. But as Quahogs. As a Quahog, you will find that new doors are open to you . . . doors that were never open to you as ordinary schmoes—"'

'Schmoes?' I raised my eyebrows. 'He called people who aren't Quahogs schmoes?'

I don't know why I was so insulted. I don't even know what a schmo is.

'May I finish?' Liam asked. 'So then he goes, "And as Quahogs you have a tradition to live up to. A tradition of greatness. There are people out there who will try to tear you down, just because they're jealous of your greatness—"'

'Wait a minute,' I interrupted with a glance at my parents. 'Are you guys listening to this?'

178

'The Quahogs *are* the top ranked team in the state . . .' Mom said. 'Maybe even the country.'

'Yeah, but *jealous of your greatness*?' I shook my head. 'Come *on*.'

'See?' Liam glared at me. 'Coach Hayes was right. You're already jealous of my greatness and I've only been a Quahog for an hour.'

'I'm not jealous,' I informed him. 'And you aren't great. And if you say that again, I'll *show* you just how not great you are.'

Liam took a single step towards me, forcing me to have to lift my chin up – *way* up – in order to look him in the eye.

'Oh yeah?' he demanded, looking down at me. 'You and whose army?'

It's so weird how much he's grown in such a short period of time. At this time last year, I'd easily been able to lift him up and throw him into the yacht-club pool. Not to hurt him or anything. Just to show him who was boss.

I couldn't help wondering who was boss now. It had to still be me. I mean, I'm the oldest.

'Ha ha,' I said sarcastically. 'That's so original. Coach Hayes obviously didn't pick you for your brains.'

'Hey, now,' Dad said mildly. He'd already wandered out to the family room, just off the kitchen, picked up the remote control and was flipping around, trying to find the golf game.

'Coach Hayes warned us about people like you,' Liam said condescendingly. 'He said the elitists in society would

179

try to make out like just because we're athletically gifted, we must be mentally deficient.'

I burst out laughing. 'Oh my God,' I said.

'Katie,' Mom said absently as she checked the messages on the answering machine – most of which seemed to be from Tiffanys and Brittanys, asking for Liam to call them back. 'Stop picking on your brother.'

'But it's like he's in a cult or something,' I said. 'I mean, *elitists in society*? Just who is that supposed to be? The people in this town who don't think just because you're a Quahog you should get extra-special treatment? I mean, beyond the corner booth at the Gull 'n' Gulp?'

'I know exactly what you're talking about, Katie,' Liam said, narrowing his eyes down at me. 'Or should I say, *who* you're talking about. And Coach Hayes had something to say about *him* too.'

'Him, who?' I demanded. Even though I knew perfectly well.

'Tommy Sullivan, that's who,' Liam boomed down at me. Ever since his voice changed, he likes making it sound deeper than it actually is. On the few occasions he's ever actually home to pick up the phone when one of the Tiffanys or Brittanys calls, he lowers his voice even more, saying, 'Hello?' in a tone so deep he sounds like freaking James Earl Jones. 'Coach Hayes said some people in Eastport would be so jealous of our greatness they'd even stoop to making up lies about us –'

I thought my head was going to explode.

180

'Tommy Sullivan may be a lot of things,' I shrieked at my brother, 'but he is not a liar!'

Unlike me.

'Oh, right!' Liam snorted in disgust. 'Give it up, Katie. Tommy Sullivan was just jealous because he knew he'd never be a Quahog, so he—'

'Oh my God,' I burst out. 'You've drunk the Kool-Aid!'

'I drank Gatorade,' Liam shouted back. 'Not Kool-Aid! I don't know what you're talking about.'

I ignored him. It was time to seek help from a higher power. Or two. 'Mom,' I said. 'Dad. Liam's drunk the Kool-Aid.'

'Stop saying that!' Liam screamed.

'Katie,' my mom said, stabbing the Pause button on the answering machine and cutting off a Brittany mid-giggle. 'Please. Don't be so dramatic. And, Liam, stop screaming. I can't hear our messages.'

'And I can't hear the TV,' Dad said, turning up the volume on his golf tournament.

'Mom,' I said, trying hard not to be dramatic. 'Would you please tell Liam that Tommy Sullivan did not make up the story about Jake Turner and those guys cheating on their SATs?'

'Yes, he did!' Liam cried. 'Coach Hayes told us all about it! He said the press is full of members of the intelligentsia, who will stop at nothing to make Quahogs look like fools because they're jealous of their athletic prowess –'

'Coach Hayes obviously hasn't seen Tommy Sullivan lately,' I muttered.

'—and that the year the Quahogs had to forfeit the state championship will forever be a black mark on the history of Eastport because of the act of one envious person—'

'That is ridiculous!' I yelled, knowing I was being dramatic again, but unable to help myself. 'Tommy didn't write that story because he was jealous! He wrote it because it wasn't fair that the Quahogs got special treatment from the proctor of that exam! I mean, they're just a bunch of football players! Why should they get to cheat on the SATs if nobody else does?'

'I told you,' Liam said angrily. 'They didn't cheat! It was a conspiracy! Coach Hayes told us so. And that's a nice way for the girlfriend of this year's team kicker to talk, by the way. I wonder how Seth would feel if he knew you think his brother's a cheater.'

'Oh, bite me,' I snarled at him.

Which is exactly when Tommy Sullivan's voice filled the kitchen. At first I couldn't tell where it was coming from. I thought he was actually there, in the room with us.

Then I realized it was a message he'd left on the answering machine, which Mom was playing back.

'*Hi, Katie,*' Tommy said, his deep voice solemn. '*It's me, Tom. Tom Sullivan. Look . . . about last night – I still don't understand exactly what happened. I – look, just call me, would you?*' Then he gave his cell number. '*We need to talk.*'

Then he hung up.

And I realized the gaze of every member of my family was on my face.

Liam was the first to speak.

'Tommy *Sullivan*?' He was sneering. He was most definitely sneering. 'You and *Tommy Sullivan*? Oh my God! Mwa ha ha ha!'

That's when I went for him.

I managed to grab a nice handful of leg hair and was tugging mercilessly – Liam screaming shrilly in pain – when suddenly I was seized by the waist from behind, and lifted straight up into the air by my father.

'My hair,' I shrieked. 'Mind my hair!'

'That is *enough*!' my father roared, setting me down again on the opposite side of the bar separating the kitchen from the family room, so that Liam and I were in different rooms. 'I have had it with the both of you! I am trying to watch GOLF!'

'She started it,' Liam said sulkily, rubbing his leg.

'*You* started it!' I yelled at him. 'You're the one who told Tommy Sullivan where I work! If you had just kept your big fat mouth shut about my private business—'

'That's it.' Mom had on her One-More-Word-And-You're-Grounded face. 'Liam. Katie. Go to your rooms.'

'I can't go to my room,' I declared. 'I have to be at my Quahog Princess pageant in –' I threw a glance at the clock. 'Oh, great. Half an hour. Now I'm going to be late.' I glared at Liam. 'Thanks a lot, nimrod.'

'Why bother going?' Liam shot back. 'You're not going to win. Not when everybody finds out who you were hanging out with last night—'

'SHUT UP!' I shrieked.

And stormed from the house.

Sixteen

I don't know how my parents can be so casual about this whole thing. I mean, this thing with my brother becoming one of *them*.

Although, now that I think about it, that's exactly what Tommy accused me of being. Right? I mean, didn't he express wonder at how I'd assimilated?

And I'd told him he was wrong, that there is no *us* versus *them*.

But according to what Liam says, Coach Hayes obviously thinks there is. And if Coach Hayes thinks that –

Oh, God, what's *wrong* with me? I've let Tommy Sullivan into my head! It's bad enough he seems to be setting up permanent occupancy in my heart (if that is the correct place for someone you can't stop thinking about kissing, and not somewhere a little more southerly). Now I've got him in my subconscious too!

It was with dark thoughts such as these that I arrived at the pageant tent. It wasn't as easy to get there today as it had been yesterday, because the park was open to the public now, and the place was packed with locals and tourists alike, enjoying the Taste of Eastport. Every restaurant in town (except the chains) had booths set up. I had to get off my bike and walk it from the park's entrance because there were too many people milling around for me to bike through.

I spied Shaniqua and Jill working at the Gull 'n' Gulp booth and gave them a wave as I pushed my bike past. They waved back and each mouthed *Good luck!*, but didn't have time to chat. The line for quahog fritters was about a mile long, and Peggy was keeping an eagle eye on the staff to make sure they didn't give the customers more than the single fritter (and dollop of sauce) their food ticket allotted.

I walked my bike towards the pageant stage and saw that a few people had already taken seats in the folding chairs in front of it. One of those people was Mr Gatch from the *Gazette*. He was smoking a cigar and playing solitaire on one of those electronic games you can get at Kmart. So I knew better than to go over and ask him, again, what Tommy Sullivan had been doing in his office.

Instead, I wheeled my bike around to the back of the changing tent behind the stage and locked it to a small sapling. I knew the workers from the parks department wouldn't like that, but there were no bike racks and all the park benches were taken by tourists digging into their quahog fritters. My bike secured, I grabbed my garment bag and lifted one of the flaps of the changing tent.

Behind it, I found bedlam. Ms Hayes was screaming at the sound guys because apparently the hand mikes weren't working and we were going to have to use clip-ons, which wouldn't work because there was no place near enough to Sidney's mouth to clip a mike, thanks to her gown's plunging neckline. Sidney was screaming at Dave, who'd apparently ordered the wrong-coloured tux from Eastport Formal Wear, and the powder blue of his jacket was going to clash with the red of Sidney's dress. Morgan was freaking out because she'd lost her rosin and was going to break her neck on the stage if her toe shoes didn't stick to it well enough.

And Jenna. Well, something had *happened* to Jenna. I didn't even recognize her at first. Her piercings were gone, as were the purple streaks in her black hair . . . which was now a pretty auburn colour and was sitting on top of her head in a gorgeous updo, with baby's breath tucked into it. She'd been stuffed into an empire-waisted lacy dress from bebe (Sidney had the exact same one, but for day, not pageant, wear) that accentuated her long, pale limbs, and on her feet were a pair of stilettos so shockingly high they were sinking into the dirt and grass beneath the chair she was sitting on. On her face she wore an expression not unlike the one hostages tend to wear after being liberated from days of captivity – dazed.

I couldn't help going up to her and being all, 'Jenna? What *happened*?'

Jenna blinked up at me. 'Oh,' she said. 'Hi, Katie. Yeah. Ambush makeover.'

Shocked, I sank down on to a nearby folding chair. 'Your mom?'

'No,' she said, shaking her head. 'My friends. They think if I win, I'll be in a position to promote their social platform.'

'Running through the streets naked covered in green Jell-O?'

'No,' Jenna said. 'Liberating the quahog. They want all quahogs to be able to live free, without fear of being dug up and eaten.'

I said, 'Jenna. Quahogs are bivalves. They aren't capable of feeling fear.'

Jenna shrugged. 'I know. But I didn't want to upset them. And whatever. I want my car back. So maybe this way, I'll place after all.'

I thought this was still pretty unlikely, given her talent (her speech includes the line, *I've SEEN the future. You know what it is? It's a forty-seven-year-old virgin sitting around in his beige pyjamas, drinking a broccoli-banana shake, singing 'I'm an Oscar Meyer Wiener'*. Pageant judges don't like it when you mention the V word in your speech).

'Wow,' I said instead. 'Does this mean you found an escort?'

Jenna rolled her eyes. 'Yeah. My *dad.*'

Still, I stood back up and laid a hand on her bare shoulder to show my solidarity with her plight. 'Fight the power, Jenna,' I said. 'Fight the power.'

Then I walked over to where Sidney was fighting with Dave just as he yanked off his powder-blue tux jacket and threw it to the ground.

'You want me to escort you shirtless?' he demanded,

caught up in a rare (for him) fit of pique. 'Fine! I'll escort you shirtless!'

Then he stomped off.

I picked up the jacket and brushed bits of grass from it.

'He can't escort you shirtless,' I said. 'It's against the rules. Escorts have to be in formal wear.'

'I know,' Sidney said. 'But *look* at that thing. It's hideous!'

'Maybe he could wear it, you know. Ironically,' I said. 'With a quahog fritter as a boutonnière.'

'Thanks,' Sidney said sarcastically. 'Not helping.'

I felt a pair of hands on my waist. I spun around to find Seth, looking gorgeous in a tux of his own – his was black, thank God – grinning down at me.

'Hey, babe,' he said, leaning over to kiss me. 'You look—'

'No,' I said quickly, reaching up to grab his face before his lips could touch mine. 'You'll mess up my make-up.'

Except that I was disturbingly aware of the fact that it wasn't my make-up I was worried about. I didn't want Seth to kiss me because . . .

. . . I just didn't want Seth to kiss me.

I know. It was insane. But at that moment, the thought of my boyfriend kissing me actually made me feel a little bit, well . . .

Queasy.

Really! I know that's a terrible thing to think about a boy. Especially a boy you've been seeing exclusively. Well, semi-exclusively.

'Sorry,' Seth said, about messing up my make-up. 'You just look so hot.'

My heart lurched. He was just so . . . sweet. How could I have treated him the way I'd been treating him lately? How?

Even though the truth is that, though Seth is *always* going on about how hot I look, he never compliments me on stuff that actually matters. Like, he's never looked at my photos and gone, 'You understand people . . . just not yourself.' He's never looked at my photos and said anything but, 'Nice. Let's make out.'

Not, you know, that I ever minded. Until fairly recently.

Oh God. What's *happening* to me?

'See, this is the tux Dave was supposed to get,' Sidney cried, grabbing Seth's jacket sleeve. 'Oh my God, your boyfriend looks so good! What is wrong with my boyfriend that he has the worst taste in all of the Eastern Seaboard? Seth, you guys went to the shop together. Why didn't you try to stop him?'

Seth looked confused . . . kind of like a puppy someone was berating for having peed on the floor. 'He thought black would be too hot,' he said. 'And he was right. I'm boiling right now.'

'So what?' Sidney shouted, loudly enough for Dave – who was over at the cooler Ms Hayes had brought along, stocked with Diet Cokes and bottled water – to overhear. 'Sometimes you have to suffer for beauty! How do you think I feel when I have my legs waxed? Do you think it feels good? Well, it doesn't. But I do it anyway, to look good for *my boyfriend*. Because I love him.'

I had no comment to make about that. I never get my legs waxed, because of the potential for bacterial infection, even at a seemingly clean salon. I use my trusty safety razor instead.

Dave had a comment though. Throwing down the water bottle he'd just chugged, he went, 'You know what, Sidney? If you have something to say to me, why don't you come over here and say it to my face instead of shouting it out for everyone in town to hear?'

Which caused Sidney to go, 'Fine, I will,' and stomp over to him.

Seth, having watched this exchange with a quizzical expression on his face, looked down at me and went, 'Wow. I guess she's really nervous about the pageant, huh?'

'I guess,' I said. I was kind of upset about the puppy thing. I mean, that I'd looked at my boyfriend's face and been reminded of a puppy. Who had just peed. That isn't the kind of thing you're supposed to think about when you look at your boyfriend. What was wrong with me? I mean, obviously Seth and I hadn't been the most perfect couple, considering I kept making out with other people (well, OK, one other person. At a time) behind his back.

But I had never thought of him as *puppyish* before. You know, cute and sweet and ultimately . . . well, kind of dim.

'Katie,' Seth said. 'Is everything OK? I mean, between you and me?'

Oh my God! It was like he'd read my mind! How'd he

190

done that? Puppies aren't supposed to be able to do that . . .

'Between us?' I asked, turning away from Sidney and Dave, who were now arguing in the opposite corner of the tent, while Morgan blubbered away about her rosin and Jenna sat there, looking as empty-headed as Katie Holmes. 'What do you mean?'

Except of course I knew exactly what he meant. I just hadn't suspected that he'd noticed.

'Well, it's like, these past few days, I've hardly seen you,' Seth said. 'I know you were sick and all, but—'

'Sick?' I blinked up at him confusedly.

'You know,' Seth said. 'Your E. coli?'

Holy quahog! I can't believe I forgot about that. I seriously have to start keeping better track of my lies. Maybe I need to make a flow chart. PowerPoint might help.

'Right,' I said. 'Well, yeah, there was that . . . and, you know, the pageant, and I've been trying to work as much as I can before school starts up again—'

'Yeah,' Seth said. 'I get all that. It's just . . . this is gonna sound kinda weird, but it's almost like . . . I don't know. Like you're not that into me any more or something.'

'Oh, Seth,' I cried, guilt twisting my heart in two. How could I? How *could* I have been so awful to him? He's such a great guy. Everybody says so.

Everybody except Tommy. For whom Seth wants to have a blanket party.

I pushed this thought resolutely from my head.

'I don't know what you're talking about,' I lied. 'Of course I'm still into you!'

Seriously. I so need a flow chart. Because the lies are just mounting higher and higher every minute.

'Oh,' Seth said, looking relieved. 'OK. Cool.'

Then he bent down to kiss me again.

And I said, ducking, 'Oops! You know what? I just need . . . I just need to step outside for a minute. I think I left something in my bike basket. Don't go away. I'll be right back, OK?'

Seth looked confused again . . . and more like a puppy than ever.

'Um,' he said. 'OK.'

I gave him a smile and hurried towards the tent flap . . . just as Eric Fluteley was lifting it to come in, looking more handsome than I'd ever seen him, in a black tux with gold studs. I braced myself, thinking he'd notice I was leaving and try to follow me out for some quick pre-pageant Frenching.

But he barely even seemed to notice me. Instead, he called to Morgan, 'Is this what you were looking for?' and held up a chunk of amber-coloured rock.

Morgan, who'd been crying (although fortunately she appeared to have applied waterproof mascara), looked up. When she saw what Eric was holding, she broke out into a radiant smile.

'Oh, *Eric*,' she cried. 'Thank you!'

And Eric blushed.

Oh yes. Eric Fluteley blushed.

192

'Excuse me, Katie,' he said when he saw me standing there by the tent flap. He stepped out of the way, courteously holding the flap up to let me by . . . though his gaze, I couldn't help but notice, was still glued to Morgan's.

Which was good. I mean, this was what I'd wanted. For Eric and Morgan to get together, because they made such a nice couple.

So I just smiled and said, 'Thanks, Eric,' and ducked outside.

Man. Nice to know how easily I can be replaced.

Well, whatever. Seth had been right about one thing: it was *boiling* inside that tent. Out in the fresh air, I felt like I could breathe again. Funny how I hadn't noticed how hot it was in there until Seth had started in with his 'Like you're not that into me any more' thing.

Which couldn't have been more out of left field. I mean, of *course* I'm into Seth.

And, all right, I'll admit it, he's not the best conversationalist. But he's still a great guy. I mean, like Sidney pointed out, he hadn't dumped me, even though I wouldn't sleep with him. That was something, right? I mean, maybe he didn't follow me home to make sure I got there safely on my bike.

And maybe he didn't exactly offer any kind of artistic criticism about my photographs.

But he's *Seth Turner*! And he's *mine*!

And what kind of idiot would ever break up with *Seth Turner*?

It was as I was thinking this I noticed a guy who kind of

193

looked like Tommy Sullivan coming towards me along the park path. Which had to have been my imagination playing tricks on me, because no way would Tommy Sullivan show himself behind the Quahog Princess pageant tent after I'd made it so explicitly clear that I never wanted to see him again.

Except when the guy got closer, I noticed he didn't just look like Tommy Sullivan.

He WAS Tommy Sullivan.

And the most annoying thing of all? When I realized this, my heart gave this kind of lurch inside my chest.

And it wasn't an *Oh no, it's Tommy Sullivan* lurch.

It was a *Yay! It's Tommy Sullivan!* lurch.

And all at once, I knew Seth was right: I just wasn't that into him any more. Because I was totally and completely into his mortal enemy.

Seventeen

'Hey,' Tommy said when he came close enough to talk to me without shouting to be heard over the shrieks of glee from all the kids running around with quahog cones (I know, gross) from the Eastport Ice Creamery. 'I've been looking all over for you.'

I just stared at him. It should be against the law for any guy to look that good. Seriously. Today he had on khaki walkshorts with a black polo.

But it wasn't even so much what he was wearing – and how well he filled it all out – as it was . . . just him.

Oh God. I had it so bad.

'I get that you want nothing to do with me,' he said. 'But can we just talk?'

I guess Tommy took my silence (which was actually speechlessness over his godlike beauty) for acquiescence, since he said, 'Good,' grabbed me by the wrist and pulled me behind the wide trunk of a sycamore tree, out of view of the pageant tent.

I went along because . . . well, what *else* are you going to do when you've pretty much lost all motor control?

'Listen,' Tommy said once he'd propped me up against the trunk of the tree (which was nice of him, since otherwise I'd probably have fallen down, my knees had gone so rubbery at the sight of him). 'What happened last night . . . I don't know what you think that was really about, but I did *not* come back to Eastport to ruin your life. I can't believe you would even think that.'

I caught myself staring at his lips as he spoke. All I could think about was how they'd felt last night on mine. And how much I wanted to grab a handful of his shirt, drag him towards me and start kissing him again, right there in Eastport Park, in front of the kids with the quahog cones, and the pageant tent, and everything.

And I could have done it too, very easily, since he had one arm up against the tree trunk beside me and was kind of leaning over me in a totally proprietary manner that I have to admit I was finding extremely enjoyable.

But then – finally – my brain kicked in, and I remembered I was supposed to hate him.

'Right,' I finally forced my mouth to say. 'So that little speech about how I don't understand – or like – myself wasn't supposed to undermine my confidence so I would screw up tonight and lose the pageant?'

He looked down at me with a totally incredulous expression on his face. 'What? *No.* Katie—'

'And that whole thing where you kissed me in the parking lot, where anyone might have seen us,' I said, folding my arms across my chest. Because I think body language is important, and I was afraid I was giving off the wrong signals with the whole letting-him-lean-over-me thing. 'That wasn't because you were *hoping* my friends would catch me and that my boyfriend would dump me and my social life would be ruined for the year?'

'Excuse me,' Tommy said, looking annoyed now instead of incredulous. 'Were we in the same parking lot last night? Because – correct me if I'm wrong – you seemed to be a pretty active participant in that kiss.'

'Ha!' I said, uncrossing my arms to stab an index finger into his chest. 'You *know* I have no resistance to cute guys in parking lots. You saw me behind the emergency generator with Eric. You were taking advantage of my only weakness, as well as acting on insider information. *And that's not fair!*'

I emphasized each of the last four words with a poke of my finger against his chest. He didn't appear to appreciate this very much, if the way he reached up and grabbed my hand was any indication.

'You're insane,' Tommy said. 'Have any of your other many boyfriends ever mentioned that to you before?'

'Don't try to change the subject,' I said, more than a little conscious that he was still holding on to my hand. 'I want to know the truth. I think I have a *right* to know it. What were you doing in Mr Gatch's office yesterday?'

'You know I can't tell you that,' he said, shaking his head.

Because it was none of my business. Mr Gatch had already made that more than clear.

'Fine,' I said between gritted teeth. Gritted in frustration because he was being so close-mouthed. Not because I was trying to keep myself from throwing my arms around his neck and kissing him again. Not at all. 'Then just tell me this: what are you *really* doing back in Eastport? And if it's not to ruin my life, then *why did you come back?*'

'Katie,' he said, looking down at my hand in his. He seemed upset. He really did. Like he wanted to tell me, but he just . . . couldn't.

Of course, that might have been part of the act. You know, the act to make me fall in love with him, then get his revenge by ripping my heart out and smearing it all over Eastport.

But I had to hand it to him. Because the act? It was totally working.

'Oh, who even cares?' I said finally, and wrenched my hand from his.

But only so I could throw my arms around his neck and start kissing him again.

Oh, yes. I was leaning against a tree in Eastport Park, kissing Tommy Sullivan behind the Quahog Princess pageant tent. Not even leaning against the tree so much as being pressed against it by Tommy, who didn't seem to mind at all that I'd ended our conversation so abruptly . . . not to mention somewhat unconventionally. Well, I guess it would have been unconventional if it had been anybody but me. But since it was me, well, what else was I going to do but kiss him?

And it wasn't like Tommy wasn't kissing me back. He was . . . and like he really meant it, I might add. His hands were on my waist, his chest pressed up against mine, his mouth hot on my mouth. In all, it was a very excellent moment.

Except that that's how long it lasted. Just a moment, before Tommy lifted his head and said in a funny, unsteady voice, 'Katie.'

'Stop talking, please,' I said, and dragged his head so that his mouth was back down where it belonged: on mine.

But he didn't keep it there long enough. For me, anyway.

'Katie,' he lifted his head to say again. 'I mean it. We can't keep doing this.'

'Why?' I demanded, dragging him down again.

But he resisted!

'Because,' he said firmly, giving my waist a little shake, 'we have to *talk*.'

'Talking is way overrated,' I said. Because, seriously, talking was the *last* thing I wanted to do with him. Especially when he was standing so close to me and I could smell his sunscreen and feel his muscles and all I wanted to do was wrap my legs around him *again*.

'Seriously, Katie,' Tommy murmured into my hair. Which I had a feeling was escaping from its updo, on account of all the bark that had just been rubbed against the back of it. 'What am I going to do with you?'

'OK,' I said. Though it was an effort to speak. On account of all the throbbing that was going on in various parts of my body. 'What do you want to talk about?'

'Us,' Tommy said. 'I don't want to do this, Katie.'

'What?' I asked, surprised. Because he certainly hadn't been acting like someone who didn't want to do this. 'Make out with me in parking lots and public parks?'

'Exactly,' Tommy said. 'That may have been all right for Eric Fluteley. But it's not all right for me. You should know up front that I'm not going to be the guy you sneak around with behind your boyfriend's back. I'm either the boyfriend, or I'm gone. So you're going to have to make a choice, Katie. It's me . . . or them.'

I narrowed my eyes as I stared up at him. Mostly I was thinking about how close his mouth was to mine and how easy it would be to just start kissing him again.

But even I, the Ado Annie of Eastport, knew that wouldn't solve anything.

Instead I tried to focus on what he had just said. Make a choice. Him or them.

Hadn't that been the exact same choice I'd had to make four years ago? Granted, we hadn't been making out behind restaurants and pageant tents back then. But it had been the same problem, really: support Tommy Sullivan and face social pariahdom forever as the class brainiac and Quahog hater. Or reject Tommy Sullivan and end up playing Spin the Bottle with Seth Turner.

How could anyone have decided otherwise?

Except that now . . . four years later . . . I couldn't help wondering: had I made the *right* choice?

Or had I just made the *easiest* one?

I blinked at him. I didn't know what to say. I needed time out. This was too hard to decide on the spur of the moment.

Tommy, almost as if he'd read my mind, reached up and touched the tip of my nose.

'Why don't you think about it,' he said. There was a trace of laughter in his voice. 'You look confused. I'll be in the audience if you want to let me know after the pageant what you've decided.'

I blinked some more. 'You're . . . you're going to watch the pageant?'

'Oh,' Tommy said with a chuckle. 'I wouldn't miss it for the world.'

'But.' Why was my brain digesting this information so slowly? 'Seth is my escort. Seth will see you. Seth might try to—'

'Well, I guess Mr Gatch will have something to report about in tomorrow's Saturday edition then, won't he?' Tommy kissed the top of my forehead, then turned around to start walking away.

And I realized, as he did so, that he'd done it again. Really. He'd rendered me a quivering mass of girly flesh with his kisses so that I couldn't think straight, and I'd just let him do all the talking. I hadn't had a chance to tell him what I thought about him and his stupid theory about how I don't like or understand myself. Which was so far from

201

the truth it wasn't even funny. I totally love myself. Hadn't I entered myself in the Quahog Princess pageant?

And I don't even *like* quahogs.

'Katie?'

I'd only staggered a few feet out from behind the tree when I heard the horrified voice coming from the tent flap. I glanced towards it and saw Sidney standing there, looking shocked.

Because she saw Tommy walking away.

Worse, Tommy saw her. And he had the nerve to wink. And say, 'How you doing, Sidney?' as he went by, around towards the front of the stage.

Sidney murmured, 'Fine, thanks.' Then, as soon as he'd rounded the side of the tent, she hobbled through the grass towards me (her heels were sinking into the soil), crying, 'Oh my God, Katie! Oh my God!'

I knew the jig was up.

And I also knew Tommy had won. He had straight up won.

It was over. *I* was over.

Weirdly, all I felt was relieved. Well, except for the part about Sidney hating me. Because the truth is, even though she's totally shallow, Sidney's always been a good friend to me. Bossy, but fun.

'Sidney,' I said. 'Look. I can explain—'

'Oh my God,' Sidney said for a third time, reaching up to pull bits of bark out of my hair. 'You look like you were just making out with some guy against a tree. Probably

202

because – surprise! – you were just making out with some guy against a tree.'

'I know,' I said gravely. 'I'm a horrible person. I guess you're going to have to tell Seth.'

'Are you mental?' Sidney wanted to know, tugging on the hem to my skirt, which had mysteriously ridden up a little. 'Get back in that tent and put some lipstick on. I don't know what you were thinking, with Mr Football Camp five minutes before you're supposed to get out on stage. Is he really that good a kisser? And how did he know my name, anyway?'

Whoa. She didn't know. She *still* didn't know.

'Huh,' I said, as Sidney grabbed my hand and started pulling me towards the tent. 'I don't know.'

'You don't know much, do you?' Sidney demanded. 'What's happening to you? Ever since this guy came around, you've turned into a total pineapple – brunette on the outside, but blonde in the middle. Don't think I haven't noticed. And how could you leave Seth alone like that? He's trapped in a corner with Jenna Hicks. She's telling him about her theories on social anarchy or something. You should know better than anyone that he has no natural defences against smart girls.'

Inside the tent, things had calmed down a little. Now that Morgan had her rosin she was all smiles, looking up at Eric in a flirty manner (hey, it takes one to know one). And Eric seemed to be eating it up (well, why wouldn't he? Anything that's all about Eric is fine with Eric).

And Sidney appeared to have forgiven Dave for picking

the wrong-coloured suit. At least if the way she went, 'I found her,' to him as she pulled me into the tent was any indication.

'Oh good,' Dave said. He was eating a quahog fritter from a tray the Gull 'n' Gulp had apparently donated for participants in the event. 'Hey, Katie. What happened to your lipstick?'

'She's reapplying,' Sidney said quickly, picking up my backpack and hurling it at me. 'Seth. I found her.'

Seth looked around from the apparently deep conversation he was having with Jenna Hicks. Which was, you know, sort of weird, on account of Seth never having once spoken to Jenna when she'd had on her eyebrow hoops.

But whatever.

'Oh,' he said when he saw me. 'Hey, babe.'

He smiled. And I waited. Waited for the gushy weak-kneed feeling I used to feel when Seth smiled at me.

I guess I shouldn't have been surprised when it didn't come. I mean, considering.

Me. Or them. That's what Tommy had said.

But isn't that what it had always boiled down to?

'Ladies.' Ms Hayes appeared from the tent flap leading out on to the stage. She looked very professional in her pink Lilly Pulitzer halter dress, with matching pink headband and shoes. 'Every seat in the house is filled. It's standing room only. This may prove to be the best attended Quahog Princess pageant in Eastport history. Get ready to give them the performance of your life.

Remember to smile. Miss Hicks, did you hear me? *Smile*. Now. Shall we pray?'

Ms Hayes didn't wait for an answer. She bowed her head, so the rest of us bowed ours too. Including the sound guys, which I thought was sweet. One of them even set down his beer.

'Dear Lord,' Ms Hayes prayed. 'Please bless this pageant and all the participants in it. Please don't let Miss Hicks mess up her blocking, and please let Miss Castle's toe shoes stick to the stage floor. And don't let Bob screw up the lighting like he did last year. Amen.'

'Amen,' we all murmured, and Morgan, for good measure, crossed herself.

'All right, girls,' Ms Hayes said brightly. 'It's *Quahog time!*'

Eighteen

OK. So it wasn't going, you know, badly. I mean, it was hot up on stage with the lights on us. And it was nerve-racking, looking out into the sea of folding chairs in front of the stage and seeing so many familiar faces . . . my parents and brother among them. In spite of the fight we'd had earlier – and the fact that it was a beauty pageant – Liam didn't look like he was having too bad a time.

Of course, that was mostly because there was a row of Tiffanys and Brittanys sitting in front of him, and all they could do was giggle and squirm and pretend to drop things so they had to lean over and pick them up and shoot him looks under their eyelashes.

Seriously. I know I am boy crazy. But if I ever thought I'd acted like that about a boy – in particular a boy as disgusting (I'm sorry, but I have smelt his feet) as my brother – I think I'd have to kill myself. Or join that Episcopalian convent I'm sure must exist somewhere.

When I looked out while Ms Hayes was giving her welcome speech and explaining about the history of the

Quahog Princess pageant (placing a special emphasis on the year she won), I could see her husband, Coach Hayes, looking pleased . . . evidently at how well the Quahog try-outs had gone earlier that day.

Or maybe he was just pleased about how hot his wife still looked, even though she was in her late thirties.

And there were Sidney's parents, Mr and Mrs van der Hoff, as well as Morgan Castle's mom and dad, beaming with pride. There were Mr and Mrs Hicks, Jenna's parents, looking nervous (they were probably familiar with her talent), Mr Hicks checking his watch . . . he was going to have to rush backstage when it was time to escort Jenna for the evening-wear segment.

I saw other people I knew as well, including Mr Bird and his wife from Eastport Old Towne Photo, and even Seth's parents, Mr and Mrs Turner. There was no sign of his brother, Jake (thank God), but that didn't mean he wasn't over at the Taste of Eastport with his friends and couldn't wander over at any moment. There were a lot of people standing at the back, including Shaniqua and Jill, who'd apparently managed to escape the Gull 'n' Gulp booth for a few minutes in order to watch.

Sitting in front of them, in the last row of folding chairs, still chomping on an unlit cigar – and still playing solitaire – was Mr Gatch.

And sitting beside him was Tommy Sullivan.

Tommy wasn't playing solitaire. Tommy was watching the action on the stage intently, with his arms crossed over his chest in that way that made his biceps bulge, and that had made Sidney elbow me while Ms Hayes was talking, and mouth, '*McHottie.*'

Which was totally true (about Tommy being a McHottie). But didn't help matters really.

Still, it was going about as well as could be expected. We got through the introductions part, and then there was the frantic stampede back to the pageant tent to change for the talent segment (except me, since I was going first). I just calmly took my place at the piano and cranked out my piece. 'I've Got Rhythm' is the only song I can play, but I play it well, because I like it. If I weren't tone deaf, I'd have sung along . . . 'Old Man Trouble, I don't mind him. You won't find him round my door.'

Except, of course, Old Man Trouble *has* been hanging out round my door. Quite a lot actually. At least, lately.

And the truth was, I *did* sort of mind him. As I played, I found myself thinking not about the fact that I was playing the piano in a pageant in front of two or three hundred people. Oh no. I wasn't thinking about that at all.

Instead, I was reflecting on the fact that if Tommy Sullivan hadn't come back to town I wouldn't even know what trouble was. Seth and I would still be making out every night after my shift at the Gull 'n' Gulp.

And Eric and I would still be making out every day before it.

Then Tommy Sullivan had come along, and it was almost as if – and this was the weirdest thing of all – I couldn't even *think* about making out with anyone else. What was *that* about?

Maybe Tommy Sullivan *was* Old Man Trouble. *My* Old Man Trouble.

And the real trouble was, I *liked* finding him round my door. What was up with *that*?

I guess my thinking about all that while I played lent some real passion to the performance, because people totally applauded when I was done. With like gusto. The Tiffanys and Brittanys even shrieked. I knew they were just doing it to show my brother that they liked me, which probably wasn't too smart of them since I wasn't high up on Liam's list of favourite people just then. But whatever. I even heard some whistling that I'm pretty sure came from Tommy Sullivan's direction.

But I ignored it, took my bow and got off the stage, so the sound guys could move the piano and Morgan could come out to do her performance of Laurie's dream sequence.

Back in the pageant tent, everyone said, 'Good job,' but, I mean, come on. It's just a song on a piano. I knew the *real* performance of the night was going to be Morgan's. Not that Sidney's Kelly Clarkson song wasn't pretty good too. But, you know.

We were sitting there listening to Morgan's toe shoes tap on the temporary stage (you couldn't really hear the music she was dancing to from where we were, because the speakers were all facing the audience), when Eric, who'd been peeking through the tent flap out on to the stage, even though Ms Hayes had told him not to, twice, went, 'Oh, my God. He's here.'

My blood turned instantly to ice, because I knew exactly who he was talking about.

But Sidney and Seth and everyone else didn't.

Which was why Sidney was like, 'Who's here?' She had already changed into her singing costume behind a set of sheets Ms Hayes had hung up in one corner of the tent for this purpose and was absently adjusting the spangled fringe on her leotard.

'Tommy Sullivan,' Eric said. 'He's sitting in the back row, next to Mr Gatch from the *Gazette*.'

There was a mad scramble for the tent flap. Everyone raced over to see Tommy Sullivan.

All except for me.

'That's not Tommy Sullivan,' Sidney declared when she'd had her turn at the flap (there was only room for one person to look at a time, if you didn't want Ms Hayes, out beside the stage, to notice you looking).

'Um, I beg your pardon, Sid,' Eric said. 'But it is.'

'It's Tommy Sullivan all right,' Seth agreed. 'I'd recognize those freaky eyes of his anywhere. Remember how they'd change colours all the time?'

'But.' Sidney turned away from the flap and towards me, her expression perplexed. 'That's the guy we saw at The Point the other day. The one you said . . .'

I shook my head at her. Just once.

I don't know if she read the panic in my eyes, or saw the way my heart was pounding through the thin fabric of my dress.

But she closed her mouth abruptly and moved out of the way to let Jenna Hicks look out of the tent flap.

'That's Tommy Sullivan?' Jenna made an appreciative sound. 'He's hot.'

'What?' Seth actually sounded offended. 'He is not!'

'Oh, he's hot,' Jenna said, straightening up and looking at Sidney and me. 'Don't you guys think he's hot?'

'Um,' I said with difficulty, my mouth having gone bone dry.

'I wouldn't know. I only have eyes for one guy,' Sidney said, wrapping her arms around the pale blue padded shoulders of her boyfriend. Dave grinned up at her. The look Sidney shot me over those padded shoulders was pointed.

'Um,' I said, still trying to summon the ability to speak. 'Me too.'

And I put my arms around Seth.

Only he shrugged them off. Because he was busy pacing.

'I can't believe he's really back,' Seth was saying as he paced. 'And that he showed up here. Here, of all places! What does he think he's doing? He's got to know he's going to get his ass kicked.'

'Hey,' I said. Which is exactly when Morgan came in through the tent flap, her performance over, and said to Sidney, 'You're up.'

Sidney squared her shoulders.

'Good luck, Sid,' Dave said, giving her a peck on the cheek. 'You're going to do great.'

'I know,' Sidney said, looking indignant – as if the thought she might do anything less than great had never occurred to her. And in truth, it probably never had – and disappeared through the tent flap.

'Dave,' Seth said as if there'd been no interruption. 'Let's call the guys and have them meet here after the pageant. We'll give Tommy a little welcome-back party.'

'Can't,' Dave said. 'You know we gotta take the girls out to celebrate when they place.' He glanced at Jenna and added, 'Sorry. No offence.'

'None taken,' Jenna said affably. 'I know I don't stand a chance.'

'The girls can wait,' Seth said, looking at me. 'Can't you, babe?'

I just stared at him. For some reason I was completely unable to speak. Morgan was the one who said something, from behind the strung-up sheets where she was changing into her evening wear.

'You guys,' her disembodied voice said, sounding disgusted. 'Why can't you just leave Tommy Sullivan alone? What did he ever do to you?'

'Everyone knows what he did,' Seth said. He actually looked kind of shocked by Morgan's question.

'Yeah,' Jenna said mildly. 'But that was like so long ago. Eighth grade or something, right?'

'And besides,' Morgan said from behind the sheets, 'he didn't even do it to you.'

'He dissed my brother,' Seth said, looking outraged. 'That's like dissing me!'

212

Jenna looked at me. 'Katie,' she said, 'you gonna help out here or what?'

But I still couldn't speak. I don't know why. I just . . . couldn't.

'I think you guys should just let it go,' Eric said. 'I mean, not that it's any of my business.'

'You're right,' Seth said sharply. I mean, for Seth. 'It's not.'

'But what do you want to go stirring up trouble for?' Eric wanted to know. 'Just let it go. You'll live longer.'

'You think that guy could take me?' Seth demanded incredulously, pointing at himself.

'Christ, Seth,' Dave said. Now he was the one peering through the tent flap, only at Sidney. 'He's right. Just let it go. It was a long time ago. OK, Sidney's done. Everybody tell her she did a good job.'

Sidney came through the tent flap, looking flushed and happy. Judging by the thunderous applause, her song had gone well. No big surprise, Sidney being perfect and all.

'Come change with me,' she said, grabbing me by the hand and pulling me towards the changing corner squared off by the hanging sheets, just as Morgan, elegant in a pure white sheath dress, came ducking out from behind them.

'Nice dress,' Sidney commented as she pulled me along behind her. 'Cavalli?'

'Armani,' Morgan said.

Sidney nodded knowledgeably. 'Cool.'

Then we were behind the protective curtains, and

213

Sidney, struggling out of her leotard, said in a low voice, 'Katie. What are you doing? I mean, seriously.'

'I don't know,' I replied miserably, wrenching off my own dress and reaching for my evening gown – a frothy pink thing Sidney had talked me into buying at Saks. 'I don't know how it happened. Honest.'

'Yeah?' Sidney's smile was brittle. 'Well, I do. But it is one thing to be catting around behind your boyfriend's back with a guy your brother met at football camp, and who's going to go back wherever he came from at the end of the season,' she said, stepping into the slinky red number she'd bought at Saks the same day I'd bought my dress. 'But it is quite another to be catting around with *Tommy Sullivan*!'

'I know,' I whispered. 'Do you think I don't know that?'

'Well, if you know that,' Sidney said, slipping her arms through the silky spaghetti straps of her gown, 'then *what are you doing it for*?'

'Do you think I *want* to be?' I whispered back. 'I can't help it!'

'Look,' Sidney said. 'This is our senior year. We've got homecoming . . . prom . . . senior trip to the city . . . tons of stuff. This is the year we're supposed to live it up, have the time of our lives, build memories to cherish forever. And how are we going to do that if you are going out with a walking dead man? Because that's what Tommy Sullivan is, Katie. Once Seth and those guys get through with him.'

'I know,' I said mournfully. 'But, Sidney, it's just that . . . I . . . I can *talk* to him.'

Sidney looked at me like I'd just said I like to eat pizza without blotting the grease off the cheese with a napkin first.

'You can *talk* to him?' she echoed. 'What is that even supposed to *mean*?'

'Well, I mean, between macking.' I knew this was going to be impossible to explain to Sidney. But I had to try. I had to try to make her understand. Because maybe if I could make her understand, I'd understand it a little better myself. 'He talks to me about . . . well, like my photography and stuff. You know Seth never does that. Seth never talks about anything. I mean, about anything besides football. And food.'

Sidney widened her heavily made-up eyes at me.

'You're only noticing that *now*?' she wanted to know. 'You've been going out since before ninth grade.'

I sniffled. I couldn't believe any of this was happening. 'I know,' I said. 'I guess I just . . . I mean, I was so flattered when he asked me – me, of all people – to go out. And then it just . . . you know. It was just how things were. Seth and I were a couple. We've been going out for so long. If I break up with him now, what will people think?'

'That you made a mistake,' Sidney said.

'*Exactly*,' I whispered painfully back.

Sidney shook her head. She looked faintly amused. 'Well. What are you going to do about it?'

'I don't know,' I said. 'Honestly, Sidney. I just . . . I don't know.'

'Well, you'd better figure it out,' she said. 'And quick.

Because if you don't, someone's going to get hurt. And I'm not just talking about Tommy. Now turn around so I can zip you up.'

I turned around. She zipped me up. Then she said, 'Good. Come on.'

And we ducked back out from between the sheets, just as Ms Hayes appeared on the other side of the tent flap and, spying Jenna, back from her performance with one hand tucked into the crook of her dad's arm, asked, 'Everyone got their escorts? All right. Good. Let's go, people. Evening wear and question time. And . . . *go*.'

'Hey,' Seth said, appearing at my side and offering me his arm. 'You look good, babe.'

'Seth,' I said. And then my throat closed up.

He blinked down at me with those sleepy brown eyes. 'What?'

I wanted to speak. I did. I wanted to say something, then and there . . .

Only I didn't know what to say. And I didn't know how to say it.

'My name's Katie,' I said instead, grabbing hold of his arm. 'Not babe. OK?'

His confused gaze turned quizzical. 'What's the matter, ba – I mean, Katie?' he wanted to know. 'Are you mad at me? What did I do?'

And I realized he was wearing that bewildered-puppy look again.

And I couldn't stand it. I really couldn't stand it a second longer. Old Man Trouble wasn't just hanging around my door.

He had set up permanent residence in my life.

I was in hell.

So of course I said, 'Nothing. Never mind,' to Seth.

Because that is what I do.

I lie.

And we went out on to the stage.

Nineteen

'Miss Castle.' Ms Hayes had made an elaborate display of shuffling the judges' questions – written down on index cards – so it couldn't be said that any one girl had been helped out by any particular judge by getting thrown an easy one. 'Please tell this audience – and our esteemed judges – some characteristics of a Quahog.'

'Certainly,' Morgan said, looking ravishing beside her equally stunning escort. I hadn't been wrong about Eric and Morgan: together, they were prettier than a wedding-cake topper.

And from the audience I'm sure you could barely tell how much Eric was sweating beneath his tux. Enough so that his pancake make-up was glistening (Eric was the only guy who'd agreed to stage make-up when Ms Hayes offered. But that's because he's used to it, on account of all his work in the theatre).

'A quahog,' Morgan began in a small voice, 'is a mollusc—'

'A little louder, dear,' Ms Hayes said in a treacly tone

completely unlike the one she'd used to yell at us during rehearsal. 'The judges can't hear you. And neither can the audience.'

'Oh,' Morgan said, lifting her mike a little higher. 'Sorry.' We were using the clip-on microphones, because the replacement hand-helds had never showed up. But because there weren't enough to go around – and nowhere to clip them on our evening gowns – we just had to hold the tiny microphones in our hands and speak into them. 'A quahog is a mollusc, and as such displays characteristics we've come to expect from molluscs, such as spitting and burying itself in the sand.'

There was an uncomfortable silence as Ms Hayes cleared her throat and glanced nervously at the judges.

'Oh, wait,' Morgan said, catching on. 'You mean a Quahog like the football players? Or a quahog like the kind people eat?'

'Er,' Ms Hayes said. 'The former, dear.'

'Oh.' Morgan back-pedalled, trying to figure out the right thing to say.

I felt bad for her. I really did. Especially since it wasn't easy even for a non-shy person to get up on that stage in front of all those people, with those bright lights shining down on us and all this pressure. Not like the Oaken Bucket was counting on Morgan to win to draw in more business or whatever.

But I'm sure Morgan needed the prize money for new toe shoes, or whatever it is ballerinas buy with prize money.

Still, it had to be even worse for her, being so shy and all.

Morgan blathered something about how Quahogs are strong and true (whatever), that was clearly designed to please the judges and seemed to work. Score one for Morgan. Actually score two, because her dance routine had been way better than anything the rest of us had done for our talent segment.

Then it was Sidney's turn, and Ms Hayes said, 'Miss van der Hoff. Can you tell me what true love is?'

Naturally, Sidney took the biblical route with her answer, since judges love that stuff. They eat it up like . . . well, quahog fritters.

"'Love is patient,'" Sidney said in her most sincere voice – the same one she uses when she's too busy partying to do her homework, so she tells the teacher her grandmother was sick and that she (Sidney) was at the hospital all night visiting her. "'Love is kind . . .'"

Yeah. Right. Try telling that to Seth. He looked super-depressed over the way I'd spoken to him just before we'd gone on stage. What had I been thinking? Why had I been so mean to him? What's wrong with me? I mean, it's true Seth's never been the shiniest knife in the drawer.

But that had seldom bothered me. Not before now.

OK, let's be honest: not until Tommy Sullivan came back.

"'Love is not rude. It is not self-seeking, it is not easily angered, it keeps no record of wrongs.'"

Huh! Unlike Seth Turner. And the thing is, it's so

bogus. Because Tommy never even did anything to *him*. All Tommy had ever done was tell the truth . . . a truth that had needed to be told, because Tommy was right: it wasn't fair that Quahogs got special treatment.

And how stupid was Jake Turner anyway, to go around bragging about cheating, and in front of an impressionable little eighth-grader? Jake Turner had ruined his own future, not Tommy.

"'Love always protects, always trusts—'"

The way Seth had always trusted me not to make out with other guys behind his back. Why did I *do* that, anyway? I mean, what was I looking for? *Who* was I looking for?

Because it's not that Seth is a bad kisser. He's an exceptionally good kisser.

Just not as good as someone else who'd kissed me recently. And I'm not talking about Eric. I mean, Seth's and Eric's kisses had never made my heart race the way a certain someone else's had. And their kisses had never made me long to wrap my legs around them. And their kisses had never made me think about them at odd random moments when I was supposed to be thinking about what drinks to pour at the soda station or where I'd left my eyelash curler.

"'Love does not delight in evil, but rejoices with the truth.'"

The truth. God, the truth. I didn't even know what the truth was any more. Except that every time I laid eyes on Tommy Sullivan, all I wanted to do was jump his bones.

It was true! Now that Tommy Sullivan had come to town, he was the only person I wanted to make out with!

"'Love always hopes, always perseveres. Love never fails.'"

Wait a minute. Wait just a minute. Is *that* what love is? Is love not wanting to make out with anybody but just one person?

And was *Tommy Sullivan* that person? Was *that* why I couldn't stand the thought of kissing Seth any more? Was *that* why I'd told Eric I just wanted to be friends?

Because I love Tommy Sullivan?

No. No, that simply isn't possible. I mean, Tommy Sullivan had only walked back into my life three days ago. How could I be in love with him when I hadn't even seen him in four years? How could I be in love with a guy who accused me of not understanding myself?

But what if Tommy's right? I mean, obviously he's right. Because LOOK AT ME. I am standing here on stage with my hand through the arm of one guy, and all I can think about is another guy.

Is that a sign of a girl who understands herself?

Oh my God. It's true. *True love is when you can't think about any guy except just one.*

Which means . . .

I'm in love with *Tommy Sullivan.*

'MISS ELLISON!'

I jerked my head towards Ms Hayes. What was she yelling at *me* for?

'Miss Ellison, I asked you a question,' Ms Hayes said,

giving me the evil eye from over the index card she held. *You are in so much trouble when this pageant is over, young lady,* her look clearly said.

'Sorry,' I said, aware that my heart was thrumming so hard inside my chest I could barely breathe. *In love. With Tom. My Sullivan,* my heart seemed to be saying, over and over again. 'Could you repeat it, please? The question?'

Ms Hayes cleared her throat. Then she read, 'Why do you, Miss Ellison, love quahogs?'

'I love quahogs for their tender succulence,' I replied automatically, while Ms Hayes, happy to see I'd recovered myself, beamed with encouragement. 'And they're especially tender . . . and . . . succulent . . . at the Gull 'n' Gulp . . .'

My voice trailed off.

Because suddenly, it hit me. Right there on the pageant stage.

What I had to do. What I had to do to get Old Man Trouble away from my door. What I had to do in order to quit lying all the time.

And so I just did it.

Because that's the other thing love is. Sidney had said it herself:

Love is truth.

'You know what?' I said, dropping Seth's arm. 'I'm lying.'

A ripple of surprise went across the audience. I saw Ms Hayes look down at the judges with an expression of befuddlement. The judges looked back at her in shock.

I knew, deep down inside, that I had just lost the Quahog Princess pageant. But I also knew, deep down inside, that I didn't care.

Because you know what? I was tired of lying. I was tired of getting caught up in my lies. I was tired of keeping flow charts and secrets. I was tired of sneaking around.

I was just tired.

'The truth is,' I said into the clip-on microphone, 'I hate quahogs.'

There was a gasp from the audience. But I didn't care.

'I do,' I went on. 'I've *always* hated them, since I was a little kid. They taste like rubber. You can do whatever you want to them. Fry them. Put them in chowder. Even make ice cream out of them. And they'll always taste the same to me. Bad.'

I was laughing. I was the *only* person present who was laughing.

But I didn't care. Because I was telling the truth.

And it felt really, really good.

'Um,' Ms Hayes said 'thank you, Miss Ellison. If you would just step back now—'

'But that's not the only thing I've been lying about,' I said into the microphone. 'Because I hate the other kind of Quahogs too. Not the mollusc. The football team.'

What went through the audience then wasn't a ripple. It was a wave. A wave of shock and resentment. All aimed at me.

But I didn't care. I really didn't.

Because I was finally telling the truth.

And it felt *good*.

'I hate football,' I said into the microphone. It was cool to hear my voice – telling the truth for once – reverberating through Eastport Park. And even if people didn't particularly like what it was saying, it still sounded like something I wasn't used to hearing – me, telling the truth. 'And I hate the way this town is about football. I hate the way we worship the Quahogs, and for what? They don't save lives. They don't teach us anything. They just chase after a stupid ball. And for that we treat them like gods.'

Now the wave wasn't just resentful. It was downright angry. Except, I noted, in the last row, where Mr Gatch had actually stopped playing solitaire and was staring at me. Beside him, Tommy's jaw was slack as he stared at me too.

'Well,' I went on, 'it's true. Don't even try to deny it. You all know what I'm talking about. We let the Quahogs get away with just about anything they want to, and if any one person tries to stand up to them – the way Tommy Sullivan did, four years ago – what do we do? We run him out of town. Don't we?'

'Miss Ellison!' Ms Hayes strode forward and tried to grab the microphone from me.

But I yanked it from her reach.

'What?' I demanded. Now my voice didn't sound so cool, I noticed. In fact, it sounded kind of shrill. Even screechy. Probably on account of the fact that I was holding back tears.

But I wasn't holding back anything else. Not by a long shot.

'We can't even SAY anything bad about the Quahogs?' I asked the audience. 'Why? They're *not* gods. They're just guys. Guys who play football. Guys who make mistakes.'

I spun around to face Seth, who was staring at me with an expression of total and complete incredulity.

'Seth,' I said a little unsteadily, on account of the tears, 'Tommy Sullivan did not ruin Jake's life. *Jake* ruined Jake's life. Jake cheated, Seth. He cheated and he got caught, and got the punishment he deserved – the same punishment any one of us would have got if we'd been caught cheating. You have got to stop blaming Tommy for what your brother did. I'm sorry. I'm so sorry. But that's how I really feel about it. I never told you before because . . . well, I guess I never even admitted it to myself before. But it's the truth. The truth about how I feel.'

Seth had been shaking his head slowly the whole time I'd been speaking. And when I finished, he gave one last final head shake and then said – with what, if I'm not mistaken, was absolute contempt in those puppy-dog brown eyes – 'If that's true – if that's how you really feel, then . . . we're *over*, babe.'

There was a gasp. It was so loud that at first I thought it had been a collective gasp from the audience.

But then I realized it had only come from Sidney.

'I know,' I said to Seth, my voice throbbing a little. 'And I'm really, really sorry.'

I meant it too. I *was* sorry. Sorry I had strung him along

for so long, sorry I was hurting him, just *sorry*. That wasn't a lie either.

Seth didn't seem like he accepted my apology though. He stomped to the opposite end of the stage and stood there with one hand over his face, like he was trying to get control over himself. After a second or two, Jenna let go of her dad's arm and went over to pat Seth comfortingly on the back. Which I thought was nice of her. If anybody could talk to Seth about living in a black well of despair and all that, it was Jenna, who claimed to have lived in one for years.

'Anyway,' I said, reaching up to wipe some moisture that seemed to be creeping into my eyes and turning back to the audience . . . and to the judges, 'I guess what I'm trying to say is, I am not – and never have been – Quahog Princess material. So you had better disqualify me. Especially because the truth is, I am not a very good example to the youth of Eastport. You see, four years ago, I—'

'NOOOOOO!' Sidney shrieked – so loudly that Dave slapped a hand over her mouth in an attempt to shut her up. He also had to grab her around the waist to keep her from hurling herself bodily at me.

'Katie!' she yelled, though her voice was muffled behind her boyfriend's hand. 'Don't!'

I said, 'Sorry, Sid,' and turned back towards the judges. The tears were flowing freely now. There was nothing I could do to hold them back.

'The truth is,' I went on, 'I shouldn't be named Quahog

Princess, because four years ago I did something – something I really, really regret. I spray-painted –'

'EEEEEEEEEEEE!!!!!!' shrieked Sidney.

'– the words *Tommy Sullivan is a freak* across the outside of the newly erected gymnasium wall of Eastport Middle School.'

The gasp that went through the audience this time had to have been heard all the way to outer space – or at least Manhattan – it was so loud.

Although I myself barely heard it, because by that time I was sobbing so loudly I couldn't even hear myself speak.

'It was me,' I cried. 'I acted alone. And I am really, really sorry.'

The minute I said I'd acted alone, Sidney shut up.

My mother, on the other hand, could be heard to let out a keening sound all of her own. No doubt because I'd just admitted something that was going to cost my family thousands of dollars.

Good thing I've got a job.

The judges blinked up at me wordlessly . . . as, behind them, did Coach Hayes. His wife had already sunk down on to the piano bench and was fanning herself with her index cards, looking as if she might pass out. Mr Gatch, in the last row, was gleefully scribbling something down in a notebook he'd brought with him.

Beside him, Tommy Sullivan – the person whose reaction to what I'd just admitted mattered most to me – seemed to be sitting frozen, just staring at me. I stared back through my tears. It was almost, in that moment, like there was no murmuring audience between us, no park around us, no parents freaking out about the cost of sandblasting an entire wall, no brother spazzing that his sister had just said she hates the team he'd only that day been selected to play on, no restaurateur groaning that I had just said I hate their main dish.

It was like it was just me, and Tommy. The way it probably should have been. If I'd been true to myself four years earlier.

'I'm sorry, Tommy,' I said into the microphone, the tears dripping down off my chin and splashing on to the pink puffy skirt of my gown. 'I didn't want to do it. I know that sounds stupid, considering . . . well, that I did it anyway. But I just . . . Well.' I shrugged. I could barely see him, the tears were coming so thick and fast now. 'Never mind.'

I looked over at Sidney, who was still being restrained from killing me by her boyfriend.

'Wow,' I said to her, reaching up to wipe away the worst of the tears with the back of my hand. 'Thanks, Sidney. I feel so much better. Love really does rejoice in the truth.'

Then I said, 'Sorry to have ruined your pageant, everybody,' to the judges and the audience. 'I'll just be going now.'

And then I dropped my microphone, lifted up my puffy pink skirt and leaped from the stage.

And ran for my bike for all I was worth.

Twenty

'So,' Jill said as we sat on the railing overlooking the water, 'you and Seth are really broken up?'

'He asked for his letter jacket back,' I said, keeping my gaze on my sneakered feet.

Shaniqua inhaled sharply. 'Harsh!'

'That's OK,' I said with a shrug. 'I think I need to take a little vacation from boys for a while.'

Jill wrinkled her nose. 'They're not all they're cracked up to be,' she assured me. 'You'll see. Try living with one.'

'I do,' I said. 'My brother, Liam – who's embarrassed to be seen with me now, by the way. Because I dissed his precious team . . . and in front of his coach.'

'I'm not talking about brothers,' Jill said.

'Yeah,' I said. 'Well, I guess maybe a boyfriend's feet stink less than a brother's do.'

'I wouldn't say *that*,' Jill said.

And just then some tourists walked up, so she had to go grab some menus and escort them to a table.

'So were your parents really mad?' Shaniqua wanted to know.

'About the seven grand they have to pay the school for the sandblasting?' I laughed. 'Oh yeah, they were thrilled. I'm grounded from now until graduation. I'm only allowed out for work, and I have to hand every penny I earn over to them until I've paid them back.'

'What about your camera?' Shaniqua cried.

I shrugged again. 'Hasta la vista, baby,' I said. I hoped she didn't notice the tremor in my voice. Also that Mr Bird wouldn't be totally crabby about giving me my sixteen hundred bucks back. Along with everything else, I'd come clean to my parents about the camera too. I'd become a veritable truth-telling geyser, as a matter of fact.

'That's not fair,' Shaniqua cried about the camera. 'You spray-painted the school so long ago! And you never would have got caught if you hadn't turned yourself in.'

'Yeah,' I said. 'Well, they don't exactly see it that way. Although my mom understands. I think. A little.'

My mom had certainly been the one who, coming home from the pageant to find me already in bed, crying as if my heart was breaking (because the truth is, I think it was), had sighed and put her arms around me and told me nothing was ever as bad as it seems. She'd even said she was proud of me for telling the truth . . . though she wished I hadn't chosen to tell it in such a public venue.

And when Liam had come in and wanted to know if he could go live at his friend Chris's house, because he didn't think he could bear the stigma of being the brother of

Katie Ellison, Quahog hater, my dad was the one who sent him to his room.

Still. Maybe things really *would* be all right. I mean, who needed friends? I had Shaniqua and Jill.

And God knew I didn't need a boyfriend. I'd had enough to last me a lifetime.

Besides, they don't let you have boyfriends in an Episcopalian convent. If such a thing even exists.

Fortunately, Peggy hadn't even been that upset about the quahog thing. When I'd come in to work the brunch shift the morning after the pageant debacle (the guy who normally worked it had called in 'sick,' suffering, no doubt, from too much Eastport Towne Fair the night before. And since I was more desperate for cash than ever, I'd agreed to cover for him), she'd merely shaken her head at me and said, 'Remind me never to sponsor another employee for anything ever again. Now go mop under the steam tables.'

Which was nice of her. For someone who'd just wanted to get rid of Old Man Trouble, I'd sure landed myself in a heap of it anyway.

And, I mean, that's OK. A liar like me doesn't deserve friends. A year in social Siberia will teach me a valuable lesson about telling the truth – not just to others, but to myself, as well.

And then maybe, after graduation, if I can't find a convent that will take me, I'll just head off to college – an all-women's college, of course – and start over.

So when Jill whizzed past me around two o'clock and said, 'Quahog alarm,' I was pretty startled. Especially when

I looked over and saw Sidney and Dave – with Eric and Morgan behind them – standing at the hostess booth.

'What do you want me to do?' Jill asked worriedly.

'They probably don't know I'm here,' I said, my heart slamming unsteadily against my ribcage. Because I could not imagine any of them – but most especially Sidney – would want to be seen at the Gull 'n' Gulp if they knew I was here too. 'I'll just go let them know. They'll probably leave.'

But when I sidled up to Sidney to ask, 'Um, can I help you guys?' she looked at me as if I were an idiot.

'Yes,' she said. 'You can get us a table.'

I blinked at her. 'Sidney,' I said. 'I'm working here today.'

'Funnily enough, I'm not blind,' Sidney said. 'I can see that.'

'Well,' I said. 'I mean, I just thought . . . maybe you'd be more comfortable eating somewhere else for a while. Because, you know . . . *I*'m here.'

'That's why we're here, Katie,' Dave said. 'To show you there's no hard feelings. Right, Sidney?' He poked Sidney in the back.

Sidney looked annoyed. 'Ow,' she said. 'Then added, 'What he said. No hard feelings. I mean, the fact that you ruined the pageant and made a total fool of yourself aside, you're still my best friend. And whatever, because I still won, which is as it should be. What do you think of my tiara?'

I looked at it. 'I think you're only supposed to wear it during the parade, Sidney,' I said.

'What, just because the parade is over, I'm not Quahog Princess any more? No way. Right, Morgan?' Sidney looked at her second runner-up, who was busy making out with Eric and so didn't seem to hear her.

'Get a room,' Sidney said again, rolling her eyes. Then, taking me by the arm, she leaned over to add, 'I called you like ten zillion times. I suppose you had your phone off again, as usual. Anyway, I wanted to say, you know . . . thanks. For not telling them the truth.'

I blinked at her. 'Sidney. I *did* tell them the truth.'

'Well, not the *whole* truth,' Sidney said. 'You know, the part about—'

'Right,' I said quickly. 'No need to say anything more about it.'

'Well.' Sidney looked uncomfortable. 'I just—'

'Really, Sid.' I looked her dead in the eye. 'No need.'

'Well. All right. I just wanted to say thanks. So. Changing the subject. Have you heard?' Sidney wanted to know. 'About Seth?'

I shook my head. It's strange, but when I hear his name now, I feel . . . nothing. Except maybe a twinge of guilt. 'No. Well, I mean, I got a message from him on my cell. He wants his jacket back. I assume that means he's all right.'

'He's fine. He couldn't join us this morning because he's hanging with Jenna Hicks.' She rolled her eyes expressively. 'Apparently, the two of them have a lot in

234

common, having the whole depression thing going for them now.'

'Well,' I said, not really very surprised. Mrs Hicks, I was sure, was thrilled. Her forcing Jenna to take part in the pageant had succeeded beyond her wildest dreams. 'That's good. I guess.'

'Yeah,' Sidney said. 'I suppose. Jenna looks good without all that nasty hardware in her face. Sort of. Anyway, there's some kind of manga convention in the city, so they're going together.'

'Manga?' I raised my eyebrows. 'And *Seth*?'

'Well, manga probably works for him. You know how he moves his lips when he reads. So, you know. Less words. What about *your* hottie? Heard from him?'

I felt my cheeks turning red. 'Um, you mean Tommy? No. No, I haven't. I don't expect to either. He's not my hottie.'

'Why not?' Sidney demanded, looking surprised.

'Sidney.' I love her. I really do. But seriously. 'I admitted last night in front of him that I spray-painted *Tommy Sullivan is a freak* on the wall of our middle school. Do you think he's really going to be that into me now?'

'Oh, whatever,' Sidney said. 'You're hot. And you're like smart. Like he is. You'd make a nice couple. So can we have our table now or what? Hey.' Her glance flicked past me. Then her eyes bulged. 'Are those *tourists* sitting there in the corner booth?'

Jill, returning to the hostess stand from showing a

235

couple to their table, looked over her shoulder at the corner booth and answered Sidney's question for her.

'Oh,' she said. 'Those are the McAllisters. From Minnesota. Nice people.'

'What are *tourists* doing at the Quahog table?' Sidney demanded.

'Oh, that's not the Quahog table any more,' Jill explained breezily. 'New restaurant policy. We voted. And we all decided that Katie is right, and it's wrong to give special privileges to any one bunch of people.' She smiled beatifically at Dave. 'Sorry.'

'No problem,' Dave, the smoother-over, said.

'But.' Sidney blinked a few times. 'What are *we* supposed to do?'

'Make a reservation next time,' Jill said, handing Sidney a beeper. 'It'll go off when a table is ready. Who's next?'

Sidney looked down at the oversized beeper in her hand. Then she looked incredulously up at me.

'Is she kidding?' Sidney wanted to know.

'Um,' I said. 'No. Sorry. But the turnover's pretty fast. Give it half an hour. I gotta get back to my tables. See you guys later.'

I hurried off to wait on my customers, unable to keep an enormous smile from my face. I couldn't believe it. Sidney didn't hate me! I actually still had a friend left at school!

That was one person, anyway . . . and a person who's pretty important to me.

236

Too bad there was zero chance of that happening with the person I *most* wanted not to hate me.

But seriously. There was no way Tommy Sullivan was going to forgive me for what I'd done. I'd seen the look of total shock on his face when he'd learned the truth.

That hadn't been the look of a man who was ready to forgive any time soon, that was for sure.

Which was fine. I mean, I just got out of a long-term relationship. I'm not getting into a new one any time soon.

Even one with a boy I'm totally positive is the right guy for me. Because I can't stop thinking about him. And his lips.

But that's wrong! Because clearly I have some growing up to do, romance-wise.

Still. I wouldn't have minded being just friends with Tommy.

If you can be just friends with a guy whose tongue has been in your mouth. Which I don't even know.

But I was pretty sure I was never going to get the chance to find out. I was willing to bet Tommy was all the way back in the city by now, leaving Eastport – and me – in his dust.

So it was a complete shock when, at the end of my shift, I walked out of the restaurant and saw him leaning against the bike rack behind the emergency generator, looking as if a fried quahog wouldn't melt in his mouth.

Twenty-One

'Wh-what are you doing here?' I stammered, stopping dead in my tracks.

'Your mom said this was where you were,' Tommy said, straightening up. 'And that you'd be getting off work about now.'

As usual, he looked incredibly good – casual in board-shorts and a slim tee. The afternoon sun, which was behind him, brought out the red highlights in his hair. I couldn't see what colour his eyes were though, because he was wearing his Ray-Bans.

He wasn't smiling. For which I didn't blame him.

'Look, Tommy,' I said, my heart slowing down to something more like a normal rhythm. It had practically leaped out of my chest at the sight of him.

But I was trying to wean myself off boys. Boys had been, after all, the root of all my troubles. Well, besides my inability to express my real opinion on things for fear of public censure.

Still, if I could just cut boys from my life permanently, maybe I'd be all right.

Although that wasn't going to be easy with Tommy Sullivan around, looking so incredibly good.

'I'm really, truly sorry for what I did,' I said. I had hoped that I might see Tommy again – just not quite this soon. Still, I had been up most of the night, rehearsing what I was going to say to him. 'I was stupid. I don't know why I—'

'You didn't,' Tommy said flatly.

I stared at him. This was not how I had rehearsed him responding. 'What?'

'You didn't spray-paint that wall, Katie,' he said, in the same flat voice. 'I know it wasn't you.'

Wait. *What?* This was *so* not how I'd rehearsed this going.

'Of course it was me,' I said, laughing incredulously. 'Why would I have stood up in front of all those people last night and told them it was me if it wasn't?'

'Because you felt guilty,' Tommy said. 'For not trying to stop Sidney and Seth and whoever else was involved in it.'

My jaw sagged. How had he known?

But I had been neglecting to tell the truth for so long about so many things, I couldn't help responding with another lie.

'That's . . . that's ridiculous,' I stammered.

Tommy just looked bored.

'I know you were *there*, Katie,' he said. 'But I also know what really went down.'

239

I stared at him again. In the distance, I could hear the Sound lapping against the sea wall, and the cry of gulls. Inside the restaurant, Sidney and Dave and Morgan and Eric had got their table, eaten and left hours ago. Sidney had made me promise to come to The Point with her to lie out by the water tomorrow, our last free day before school started. She had even invited Morgan along as well, a display of graciousness I knew was a direct result of her being the new Quahog Princess.

Now, in the lull between the brunch and dinner shift, the line cooks in the kitchen had turned the satellite radio to the eighties station, because Peggy had gone home. The speakers were pounding Pat Benatar.

But close up all I could hear was my own breathing.

'What are you talking about?' I demanded, ignoring the feeling of tightness in my chest. 'How could you know any of that? Unless—'

'Unless I was there that night? I *was* there that night,' Tommy said, still looking bored. 'I was on my bike, over by the side of the building. You guys didn't see me. But I saw you. And I heard them. And what they were going to write.'

'Tommy.' My heartbeat had sped up again. Because this was awful. This changed everything. This –

'And after Seth sprayed the letter F,' Tommy said, 'you grabbed the spray can away from him, and you wrote –'

'– freak,' I finished for him, my eyes closed.

'Right,' Tommy said. His voice sounded strange. I couldn't figure out why. But even though I'd opened my eyes, I didn't dare raise my gaze and risk glancing at his

240

face. Because I knew what the sight of those amber eyes – even behind such dark lenses – might do to me. To say nothing of his lips.

'I always wondered why you did that,' he said. 'Why *did* you do that, Katie?'

'Because,' I said. I wanted to cry all over again. Like I apparently hadn't cried enough last night, weeping on my mom's shoulder – and then, after she'd gone to bed, into my pillow – half the night. I kept my gaze on the gravel at my feet.

It was time to tell the truth. The *whole* truth.

'I couldn't let him write what he'd been going to,' I said. 'Seth, I mean. But I couldn't stop him from finishing what he'd started. So I grabbed the can and wrote something else. Oh, what does it *matter*, anyway?'

'It matters,' Tommy said in the same quiet voice. 'It's always mattered. To me, anyway. Whenever things got really bad – and they did get really very bad – I'd think about what you did. And I'd wonder why you did it.'

'Because you were my friend,' I said quickly. The tears weren't just gathering under my eyelashes now. They were starting to spill out from under them. Frustrated – because I didn't want him to see I was crying – I turned around and plunked down so that I was sitting on the bike rack.

'Was that what we were?' Tommy asked.

And now I knew what that thing was in his voice, that thing I hadn't been able to put a name to until now. It was bitterness.

And it made me cry out, 'Yes, of course! I may have

241

been a crappy friend to you, Tommy. But I was still your friend. I *wanted* to do right by you. As much as I *could* do, in my admittedly limited capacity.'

'Hey.' Now Tommy's voice was gentle. I still couldn't look up at him – because I was ashamed of my tears. But I could see his feet move into my sight range. He was wearing black suede Pumas. 'Katie. You've got the wrong idea. I never blamed you. I thought it was cool, what you did . . . changing the intended word to freak. I could handle being a freak.'

'Then . . . why did you leave town?' I asked his feet.

'Because my parents couldn't handle having a son who's a freak,' he said with a laugh. And the next thing I knew, he was sitting on the bike rack next to me – though I was still careful not to look into his face. 'They didn't think it was good for me to be in Eastport. They wanted me to get a good education, not be worrying all the time about people spray-painting my name on buildings. So they pulled out. It was probably the right thing for them to do. Who knows?'

I said, still unable to raise my gaze higher than his knees, 'But then . . . why did you come back? And *don't* say you can't tell me. Because otherwise I'm going to know it's to get revenge on me. Which you've managed to do, and pretty good. The whole town hates me now. Practically.'

'Nobody hates you,' Tommy said. Now there was laughter in his voice. 'Except Seth, maybe.'

'Seth definitely hates me,' I said, thinking mournfully of his terse message asking for his jacket back.

'Yeah, well, Seth always was an idiot,' Tommy said. 'Just like his brother, he wants to blame everybody else for his own mistakes.'

'I *was* a jerk to him though,' I admitted sadly. 'I was a pretty big jerk to you too.'

'You weren't a jerk,' Tommy said. 'You were just freaked out. About starting high school with everyone hating you. I think it was natural to want to distance yourself from me.'

'Really?' I risked a glance at his face, trying to gauge the bitterness level.

But all I saw was his smile. Which made my heart lurch.

And of course, after that, I couldn't look away.

'Yeah,' he said grinning. 'But you redeemed yourself last night. That was quite a speech.'

'Not really,' I said, chewing on my lower lip. Because I hadn't been able to avoid noticing that, in the light from the afternoon sun, Tommy's own lips looked particularly inviting.

What was *wrong* with me? Why didn't my body seem to know that my brain had sworn off boys? For good.

'Don't be so hard on yourself,' Tommy said, bumping his shoulder against mine.

He meant it, I knew, as a friendly gesture. He didn't do it to make electric shocks of desire go shooting through me.

But that's exactly what happened.

Which is why I looked away from him and said, 'I'm taking a vacation from guys,' as fast as I could. Because I was reminding myself – as well as letting him know – that physical contact, even shoulder bumping, was off the menu.

'Really?' Tommy *definitely* sounded amused now. I had to risk another glance at his face, just to see if he really was laughing at me.

He was.

And he still looked hot as ever.

My cheeks burning, I hunched my shoulders and looked away from him again.

'It's not funny,' I said to the tops of my sneakers. 'You were right. I need to learn to understand myself better – and, like you said, *like* myself better – before I get into any more romantic relationships. Telling the truth for a change is a start. But I have a long way to go.'

I decided against telling him about Phase Two of my plan . . . the convent and/or all-women's college. Better to take it one day at a time at this point.

'That sounds like an excellent plan to me,' Tommy said.

My shoulders slumped a little. I don't know why I was so disappointed by his response. I guess I hadn't exactly thought he'd try to talk me out of it.

But I thought he'd at least have said something like, *Too bad. I was about to ask you out.*

But this is just an example of how much I really do need to take a vacation from boys.

'I'll let you in on a secret, if it'll cheer you up a little,' Tommy went on. 'It's about why I'm back in Eastport. Well, part of the reason. But it's got to stay a secret till tomorrow morning. So you have to promise not to tell.'

'OK,' I said, instantly curious.

He reached down and pulled up a backpack that had been sitting in the gravel near my bike. Unzipping it, he took out a newspaper. I recognized the standard for the *Gazette*. It was the Sunday – tomorrow's – edition.

'Turn it to the Sports Section,' Tommy said.

I did. And was shocked by what I saw.

'That's you!' I cried.

Because it was. There was a new column along the left-hand side of the page – the high-school sports beat. And there, next to a byline that read Tom Sullivan, was Tommy's picture.

'*That*'s what you came back for?' I cried. 'Because Mr Gatch offered you the high-school sports beat?'

'Well, partly,' Tommy said. 'But you can see why I'm not too worried about those guys – what did you call it? Oh yeah – having any kind of blanket party for me. I don't think Coach Hayes – or anyone else for that matter – would take too kindly to the Quahogs beating up the reporter who's going to be covering their games all year.'

'Tommy,' I breathed, looking down at his photo. He looked totally great in it. Maybe I'd cut it out, and when I was living in the convent I could look at Tommy's photo and remember what it was like to be kissed by him. 'This is . . . this is really impressive. It really is. Mr Gatch has never hired anyone as young as you before. I mean, to have their own column.'

'Yeah,' Tommy said. 'It was a pretty strong incentive to come back, I'll admit. My parents weren't too thrilled about it, but when I explained how good it would look as part of my college applications, they finally agreed to let me give it a try.'

'Well,' I said. I handed the paper back to him reluctantly. 'I, um. I guess I must have sounded really stupid, going on about thinking you were here because of . . . well. Me.'

'Not *that* stupid,' Tommy admitted with a smile, as he stuck the paper back into his bag. 'Because you were partly right.'

I blinked at him. 'What do you mean?'

'Oh, hey, I almost forgot,' he said, ignoring my question. 'I have something of yours.'

'Of mine? What?'

And he reached into the backpack again, and this time drew out something bulky, wrapped in a brown paper bag.

'What is it?' I asked, taking hold of it curiously. 'What –'

But the minute my fingers went round it, I knew.

'Tommy!' I cried, springing up from the bike rack and pressing the thing in the bag to my heart. 'No. You didn't.'

My mouth said the words. But my hands, clutching the camera to me, said something else entirely – they said, *Mine*. Because it was like they were home.

'You're right,' Tommy was grinning. 'I didn't. Mr Gatch did. Well, he and Mr Bird, really. You know how much they both hate the Quahogs. Oh, and here.' Tommy reached into his backpack and pulled out an envelope, which he slipped into my hands. 'Your money back. So you can give it to your parents, to put towards the sandblasting.'

I just shook my head in wonder. The tears had come back.

But they were a different kind of tears from before.

'Tommy,' I whispered. '*Thank you.*'

'Don't thank me. And don't think you're getting that camera for free, either. Mr G expects you to work it off taking photos for the paper this year. I was hoping you'd cover the games with me. What do you say?'

I shook my head some more. 'Tommy . . . why? I mean . . . why are you being so nice to me? After what I did?'

He shrugged, getting up from the bike rack. 'Are you kidding? *I'*m the one who owes *you*. If it weren't for me, you'd have placed in that pageant last night. Jenna Hicks only placed because you dropped out.'

Which was when I noticed something, despite my tears. Or rather, I noticed something missing. From the Gull 'n' Gulp parking lot.

'Tommy,' I said, blinking back the tears. 'Where's your Jeep?'

'Oh,' he said. He had bent over to unlock a chain around a mountain bike parked beside mine. 'Back at my grandparents' place. I figure, you know, if we're going to be hanging out, I'm better off with pedal power if I'm going to keep up with you.'

I just looked at him. When he'd successfully removed the chain, he straightened up and noticed my stare.

'What?' he asked, looking puzzled. 'You wouldn't get in my car anyway.'

'Tommy.'

My heart was beating slowly and steadily beneath the Leica I was pressing to it. It wasn't fluttering. It wasn't hammering. It was just thumping. Ka-thump. Ka-thump.

'What you were saying before, about why you came back.' I licked my lips, which had gone dry as the gravel beneath my feet. 'You said I was partly right. That it was because of me.'

'Oh,' Tommy said, his gaze on mine. 'That.'

I didn't look down this time. I looked right into those amber-gold-green eyes of his.

'Yes,' I said. Ka-thump. Ka-thump. Overhead, a seagull screamed. 'That.'

'Well, I'll admit,' Tommy said finally. 'I was curious.'

Ka-thump. 'About what?'

'About whether or not I was still in love with you,' Tommy said.

KA-THUMP.

'You were in love with me?' I echoed. 'You mean . . . in the eighth grade?'

'You sound shocked to hear it,' Tommy said wryly. 'I guess I hid it pretty well.'

'*Super* well,' I said. Ka-thump. And, in spite of all my best intentions, I found myself taking a step towards him. 'I had no idea.'

'Well, you were pretty hot, even then,' he pointed out. 'I don't know if it was the braces or the frizzy hair that did it.'

KA-THUMP.

'Was that what the peanut-butter cookies were all about?' I asked, taking another step towards him.

'Absolutely,' Tommy said. 'My plan was to lure you into my romantic clutches with Scholastic Reading Counts quizzes and peanut-butter cookies. Not very sophisticated, but the best I could come up with at the time. It was eighth grade, after all.'

One last step and I was standing directly in front of him, so close that I had to tilt my chin up in order to look into his eyes. With his sunglasses on, I couldn't see what colour they were just then. But I was betting bright, ocean green.

'And?' I asked.

He looked down at me, his gaze unreadable, thanks to the Ray-Bans.

'And what?'

'And *are* you still in love with me?' I asked.

He grinned. 'What do you care? I thought you were taking a vacation from guys.'

'I am,' I assured him. Goodbye, convent. Goodbye, all-women's college. 'From every guy but you.'

Which is when he took his sunglasses off. And I saw that his eyes were bright green, just as I'd suspected they'd be.

'In that case,' he said, 'the answer is yes.'

But the truth is, I'd already forgotten what the question was. Because I was too busy kissing him.

A selected list of titles available from Macmillan Children's Books

The prices shown below are correct at the time of going to press. However, Macmillan Publishers reserves the right to show new retail prices on covers, which may differ from those previously advertised.

All Pan Macmillan titles can be ordered from our website, www.panmacmillan.com, or from your local bookshop and are also available by post from:

Bookpost, PO Box 29, Douglas, Isle of Man IM99 1BQ

Credit cards accepted. For details:
Telephone: 01624 677237
Fax: 01624 670923
Email: bookshop@enterprise.net
www.bookpost.co.uk

Free postage and packing in the United Kingdom